Praise for

THE BRIDE
CLOSED THE DOOR

"Ronit Matalon was a giant of Israeli literature: not of the bombast of grand political statements, but rather a master of the private, the intimate, the ambivalent, the human. *And the Bride Closed the Door* invites us into a single revealing moment in a family's life, and we are right there in the room with them—or rather, right outside the door. It's funny, moving and deeply real." —DARA HORN,
author of *Eternal Life* and *Guide for the Perplexed*

"Refreshingly audacious and stirringly sophisticated, *And the Bride Closed the Door* presents the reader with a sharp-edged piece of social and feminist critique, hidden by a veil of wit and humor. Jessica Cohen's masterful translation further enhances the rare and intricate voice of Ronit Matalon, one of Israel's leading female authors, whose sudden passing shocked and saddened lovers of Hebrew literature worldwide."
—RUBY NAMDAR,
author of *The Ruined House*

"With seductive wit and light pathos, this brilliant novel makes the reader privy to the inner thoughts of a comically messy family. From there, bigger truths about personal life and the wider culture are exposed and explored."
—BETHANY BALL,
author of *What to Do About the Solomons*

"*And The Bride Closed the Door,* translated masterfully by Jessica Cohen, is a triumph, at once humorous and profound, richly imagined and deliciously grotesque. The bride in question—as brilliant, rebellious and intriguing as Matalon herself—remains absent throughout the book, and revealed only through the eyes of a colorful cast of characters who try and coax her out of the locked room. Whether you read it as an allegory or a comedy, this book is a marvel, a stunning display of Matalon's virtuosity and an aching reminder of the tremendous void she left behind."　　　　—AYELET TSABARI, author of *The Art of Leaving*

"A fable of the Israeli condition . . . Matalon is one of today's best Israeli authors, one of the original, intriguing and unique voices now active here. Her writing—the themes, the characters, the way they are shaped—is distinct and unique."
—*HAARETZ*

"A remarkable book. The deep inner structures of Israeli society, the existential tensions of being Israeli, and questions pertaining to the definition of individual identity are dealt with brilliantly and light-handedly."
—THE BRENNER PRIZE COMMITTEE, 2017

"It remains unclear whether this novel is an allegory of hopelessness or a feminist manifesto. The narrative allows for many interpretations and perhaps most importantly it's a comedy."
—*FRANKFURTER ALLGEMEINE ZEITUNG*

"Ronit Matalon, a major figure in Israeli literature who died in 2017, exposes the contradictions of her country."
—*L'EXPRESS*

AND THE
BRIDE
CLOSED
THE DOOR

RONIT
MATALON

TRANSLATED FROM THE
HEBREW BY JESSICA COHEN

NEW VESSEL PRESS
NEW YORK

New Vessel Press

www.newvesselpress.com

First published in Hebrew in 2016 as Ve-Ha-Kala Sagra Et Ha-Delet

Copyright 2019 © by The Estate of Ronit Matalon

Published by arrangement with The Institute for the Translation of Hebrew Literature

Supported by "Am Ha-Sefer"—The Israeli Fund for Translation of Hebrew Books,
The Cultural Administration, Israel Ministry of Culture and Sport

Translation copyright © 2019 Jessica Cohen

Library of Congress Cataloging-in-Publication Data
Matalon, Ronit
[Ve-Ha-Kala Sagra Et Ha-Delet, English]
And the Bride Closed the Door/ Ronit Matalon; translation by Jessica Cohen.
p. cm.
ISBN 978-1-939931-75-7
Library of Congress Control Number 2019934494
I. Israel—Fiction

For my son, Daniel

The young bride, who had been locked in her room in utter silence for more than five hours, finally made her announcement, then repeated the astonishing declaration three times from behind the closed door, through which four pairs of ears listened anxiously and with the utmost devotion. "Not getting married. Not getting married. Not getting married," she recited in a flat, almost bored voice that sounded extremely distant and nebulous, like the final vapors of a scented cleaning spray.

Three of them were crowded into the sad hallway (the grandmother had been placed upon a wicker stool opposite the door when her feet had grown weary from the long wait) and avoided looking at one another for a long time, as though any eye contact might turn the declaration they had just heard into a solid fact, confirming not only its content, but worse—its significance. And so they simply continued to stare at the shut door with its old-fashioned dark wood veneer, seemingly anticipating a thawing, a softening, a miraculous melting—if not of the bride then at least of the door—and hoping for something further: a continuation of the sentence, an idea or a word that might emerge through the door like the wet head of a newborn closely followed by the body itself sliding out.

"I'm cold," said the bride's mother, Nadia. She tried to encircle her fleshy shoulders with her own arms, which were encased in the tight-fitting, prickly lace sleeves of the light gray evening gown she had been trying on, at the hairstylist's request, though her feet were absentmindedly clad in plaid winter slippers with zippers down the front. Her dyed blond quiff perked up in surprise over her forehead, and similar wonderment veiled her gaze when it unintentionally fell on the grandmother, her own elderly mother, by whose presence she seemed as perplexed as she might be by an unfamiliar piece of furniture that she had not ordered yet was suddenly delivered to her home.

"What did Margie say?" the grandmother asked cheerfully. She was hard of hearing and generally "not with us," as Nadia put it, and throughout all these hours of waiting she had sustained a dazzling smile, full of the pearly white teeth inlayed by the dentist only a week earlier, in honor of the wedding. "What did she say?" she repeated, hanging her round gaze on the chrome door handle, which was positioned precisely at her eye level. She sat on the stool with her legs obediently straight and close together, like a kindergartener at circle time, and patted the remaining two apple quarters (two she had already eaten) on a dish towel on her lap.

Nadia leaned over and gripped her elbow: "Go on, go rest in the living room for now. We'll let you know when there's any news."

The grandmother munched on some apple, and a thin dribble of pale yellow juice ran from the corner of her mouth down to her chin. "Booze? What booze? They'll have plenty of drinks at the catering hall, don't worry," she assured them, wiping her fingertips on the dish towel.

The phone rang in Matti's pocket. He quickly silenced it, but a few seconds later it rang again and he turned it off yet again. "It's not her?" asked Nadia. "It's not her," the groom replied, "I have her phone, did you forget?" Nadia closed her heavily made-up eyes. "I didn't forget. I didn't know you had it. How could I forget something I didn't know?" She paused. "What are we going to do?" Then she repeated her question more quietly, as if trying not to wake someone: "What are we going to do?"

Matti looked at her intently, somewhat wistful yet completely alert, and seemed to be considering her question, although he wasn't really. She could feel his gaze jabbing her in the spot right between her painted eyebrows with an injection of despair, tense expectation, and something else she couldn't quite name. Startled, she turned sharply to Ilan, her nephew, who was leaning over on her right and whispering in her ear. "What? What did you say?" Nadia was confused.

"I corrected you. I said: '*God*, what are we going to do?' That's what I said you should have said. 'God, what are we going to do?'" Ilan displayed his ugliest sneer, intentionally exaggerated, then went back to covetously playing with Nadia's six gold bracelets. He rolled them up and down her arm, counted them over and over again, pulled them almost up to her elbow then dropped them back down, one by one, to her wrist.

"What does God have to do with it?" Nadia pulled her arm away impatiently. "Why would you bring God into this?"

"It's true. God forgets no one. *Allah ma biyinsash khad*, like they say," the grandmother announced with contemplative satisfaction, rocking slightly from side to side on the stool to stretch her buttocks. Nadia put her hands over her eyes. "I can't take her. I can't. Explain to her what's happening," she murmured at Ilan without looking at him, and leaned her back against the wall.

Ilan wiped his dry hands on his pants, moved closer to the grandmother's stool, knelt down before her with his eyes straight across from hers, cupped her milky cheeks in his hands and held her head right in front of his own, so that she could watch his lips move. "Gramsy!" he said quietly, in a soft but persuasive voice. "Lena!" The grandmother's face lit up and her wide nostrils trembled slightly with joy, as though her name pronounced by Ilan were a surprising discovery. "Can you hear me, sweetie?" he asked with a grave look. She nodded vigorously. "It's Margie. *Mar-gie.* She's not getting married in the end," he explained. "Why not?" the grandmother asked, as a look of confusion and dread spread over her face. "Why isn't she getting married?" Ilan replied slowly, accentuating every syllable: "She doesn't want to. She said she doesn't want to get married." "Ever?" the grandmother inquired. "She doesn't ever want to get married?" Ilan reached out, stroked her hair, and tucked a long strand behind her ear. "I don't know if not ever, sweetie. We don't know. For now—she doesn't want to get married."

Nadia cried out. For the first time in the past half hour, the news sank in and hit her all at once, suddenly embodied in Ilan's words, which ruptured her with their tenderness far more than a whip or a violent shaking could have. Her neck was bent forward and the skin was flushed, her hands covered her ears, and she gaped, extricating from inside her body a peculiar, truncated, almost inhuman wail, which she herself had never heard before. As she yelled (and now she also began striking her thigh rhythmically with her right hand) she marveled at this voice, so horrifyingly foreign, which was apparently coming from inside her, just as if her body and mind had split into two—two women: one screaming until her facial muscles ached and her eyes burned, and the other casually filing her nails and throwing the occasional curious glance at the screaming one.

The screamer was the one who turned to the door and began to pound on it (the enormous amethyst ring on her finger pivoted into her palm and injured her): "Open up, Margie! Open up! Do you hear me? Open the door now or this is the end of you! The end, do you hear me? What's the matter with you? What? What are we supposed to tell people? Five hundred people in that wedding hall four hours from now with the food and the band and everything! What are we going to tell them? What will they think of us?" Then she turned to Matti, one hand still banging on the door with feeble acquiescence, and added, "I had a feeling all morning. All morning. When she got up this morning and said she wasn't going to the bridal salon. That we should cancel with the salon. With that face she had as soon as she got up, I knew, but I didn't want to know, you see? I was afraid to know what that face meant." She touched her red, painful hands, then wrenched the amethyst ring off and flung it furiously at the bathroom.

Ilan leapt up, crawled over to the little bathroom, and felt around the floor for a long time until he found the ring behind the toilet. He spat on it, wiped it off thoroughly, and held it out to Nadia: "Here. Isn't it a shame to throw away such a beauty because that basket case locked herself in her room? Isn't it a shame?" Nadia wept softly and shook her head over and over again, mechanically. Her face was twisted under a caked mask of makeup, and the blond quiff clung to her damp, painted eyelashes, its tips smudged black from the mascara. She shrugged her shoulders, wiped her eyes on the hem of her dress, and pushed Ilan away. "Don't bother me with that ring now. Nothing but rotten luck it's brought us. Only rotten luck." Ilan stared, transfixed, at the pale purple stone, then hesitated, held the ring to his lips, and put it on his finger. "I'll take care of this stunner for you. Don't you worry, I'll take care of it like I care for my own eyes," he promised.

Ilan, who was twenty-one, regarded his dazzling green-gray eyes as his greatest, most secure asset. Almost no one—including himself—could resist their allure, and for years (since the age of ten or so) he had compulsively followed a ritual of examining his face in the mirror at length, then emitting a resigned sigh, as if to reluctantly acknowledge: Can't do anything about it—these eyes are so gorgeous they could drive a person crazy.

Outside the realm of his eyes, Ilan found things less satisfactory, and this caused him constant but silent suffering. His long, thin body seemed as though it were being stretched on either side by unequally matched powers, each struggling to pull the hardest. His vexing proportions were clearly the result of this struggle: from the waist up, his physique brought to mind a long noodle of dough that had been rolled, stretched, and thinned until his rear end had the same degree of flatness as his back, while his head and squashed face, particularly when viewed frontally, looked like the direct continuation of his neck in one straight line. His legs, on the other hand, were as short as a child's, and the feet protruding from them were abnormally narrow, extremely long (he wore a size 12), and embarrassingly pale, or so he felt, which was why he never dared wear sandals.

After his parents divorced, Ilan had moved in with Gramsy (a nickname he had invented when he was three), who lived in a one-bedroom apartment next door to Nadia. He slept on a narrow twin bed in a closed-in balcony off the kitchen, surrounded by piles of empty boxes, broken lamp shades, and various tatters left behind by the previous tenant. (Gramsy was terrified she might return at any moment to demand her pathetic but legal belongings). There were muslin blouses from the 1940s with missing buttons and frayed seams under the arms, which had once been white but were now yellow; moth-eaten ball gowns in lavender and baby-blue chiffon with high, narrow waistlines; a faux fur stole covered with a thin layer of glue and dead bugs; pink corsets with dozens of hooks; and one black silk nightgown that had survived virtually intact apart from its completely disintegrated train, which Ilan cherished above all the other items in this legacy that he viewed as his own. He tried on the nightgown every evening, marveling at its décolletage (a word he had learned from Gramsy), which was adorned with two rows of colorful crystal stones that he affectionately called "my candy."

Ilan was exempt from military service due to "incompatibility," though he insisted with fearsome resoluteness—or with smug indifference, depending on his mood—that it was not he who was incompatible with the army, but rather the army that was incompatible with him. (He had once heard that line from someone, and pretended—then later forgot that he was pretending—that he had come up with it.) The issue of military service seemed to come between him and Matti, whom Ilan perceived as the embodiment of "the establishment." Whenever their paths crossed, above every word Matti said, every "pass the Coke please, Ilan," there hovered, in Ilan's mind's eye, a giant, colorful neon sign flashing the word *A-R-M-Y* while an imaginary siren blared. This vision aroused contractions of terror, distress, and latent anger, which gripped Ilan in the diaphragm and dysregulated his breath.

This was what he experienced as he stood in the hallway wearing Nadia's amethyst ring on his finger and his eyes met Matti's and encountered one of those looks—the supposedly hesitant looks that embodied a dark core of hostility, which passed through Ilan's face, penetrated his mind, and exited out the other side of his head, transmitting a momentary tremor through his thin, weak hands. He fled to Gramsy, dabbed the saliva and apple juice off her chin with the dish towel, and kept his back to Matti ("that guy," as he privately called him), which meant that he hardly heard

Matti speaking, imbuing his voice with a firm courtesy that sounded very foreign.

"I want you all to leave, please. Leave us alone." Matti's words finally broke through. He took off his jacket and slung it over his arm as though preparing for a long walk.

"Which us? Us who?" asked Nadia.

"Us. Me and Margie," Matti replied. Then he glared at the door and waited, his back turned to them. His body looked rigid and poised, as if it had been wrapped in cling film. He stood there until the final sounds and rustles attested to their departure.

Matti put his ear against the door and listened for a long time. The ticking of the large wall clock (an employee gift from Koor Industries years ago) came from inside the room, very faint in the silence. He bent down, peeked through the keyhole, and his eye came up against a dark spot that must have been the key stuck in the lock from the other side of the door. "Margie!" he called, shuddering slightly from the unfamiliar sound of his own voice. Then quietly, "Margie? Are you there?" He waited, gazing down at the pointed toes of the new black patent leather shoes Margie had talked him into buying.

As he stood there, captivated by the glimmer of his shoes, that incident in the shoe store with Margie a week ago suddenly forced itself on him, compelling him to recall and recount its every detail, now of all times: how he and Margie had taken a taxi to the store at the north end of Dizengoff Street in Tel Aviv (his car was in the shop), how Margie's feet hurt from the new shoes she'd just bought and insisted on wearing immediately, how they'd looked for a pharmacy to buy Band-Aids, paid and left the box on the counter, gone back to the pharmacy again (and the argument that had ensued at a street bench on which Margie collapsed, over whether to go back to the pharmacy where they'd left the Band-Aids or buy new ones at a closer pharmacy; and the beads of sweat on Margie's chin when she barked, "It's pennies, Matti! Those Band-Aids cost pennies, for God's sake!") and then the taxi. No, actually before the taxi and before the pharmacy, they'd stopped for ice cream. She didn't like hers (pistachio), had been tempted by the pale green color but after a few licks she wanted to throw it away. And then the taxi. Margie's long, brown thigh slung distractedly over his, and what she said while she gazed out the window, not at him. "I love taking cabs so much. Being driven. I wish this would never end," she'd said, and all at once Matti felt so abandoned, but he didn't respond, simply tried to quell the buds of displeasure and disappointment inside himself, even though he did not fully understand what she meant, and privately wondered whether to be hurt by her absent-mindedness, which projected such anonymity, or to just let it be, to just leave it.

He remembered her protruding kneecap when she'd placed her leg on his thigh in the taxi and rubbed her sore heels. Margie's sharp, bronzed kneecap with the thick scar from when she'd fallen off her bike at age seven. He remembered how she'd told him about that fall, when she'd rolled down the street with the bike. She was lying on the side of the road, her arms and knees bleeding, and when a woman walked by and wanted to help, she'd told her, "Don't do me any favors." There was enormous wonder in him now at that "Don't do me any favors," which she'd recounted to him with both disgust and pride. It was a completely different species of wonder, so much deeper than the previous one, from two years ago, when she'd told him the bike story and his wonderment had been somehow tempered with bemusement.

And then there was the men's shoe store. The grooms' store, to be precise. And the salesclerk, at once obsequious and indifferent, who had aroused a strange loathing in Matti. The moment of embarrassment when he took his shoes off and discovered a hole in one sock, which he put his hand over. How he'd been embarrassed in front of Margie and how she'd suddenly put her arms around him (a moment earlier she'd been completely absorbed in her broken thumb nail, and he'd felt clumsy and superfluous in the store's fragrant air), put her lips on his neck and whispered, "I saw your shame."

Just then the clerk came over with those patent leather shoes, the ones Margie had seen in the window before they'd walked in and had clapped her hands delightedly. He'd given her a sideways glance, suspicious yet enchanted by her childish excitement ("Matti, don't say 'childish' any time you don't understand something," she'd once scolded him), and as they'd walked through the store's automatic doors he'd told her, "You . . . Anyone can buy you with all that glittery stuff, just like the Indians," but she didn't hear, she was already talking to the salesclerk, who treated her with esteem, having figured out instantly who had the power and who made the decisions in this couple.

Was that what irritated him so much when he rejected the shoes, pushed the box back at the clerk, laced up his own shoes, and stormed out of the shop? Margie was in no hurry to follow. Not in any real hurry. He remembered the moments he'd spent standing outside, next to a glass recycling bin, slightly embarrassed by himself, almost choking from the way she'd hurt him by not hurrying out after him. He repeated to himself over and over again what he planned to say to her, or rather to hurl at her: "I'm not a doll that you dress up in flashy shoes, do you understand?" Each time he recited the line and reached the crescendo— "understand?"—with its rhetorical, echoing question mark, he felt the blood pulsing in his temples. Pulsing, that was the word. What the hell was she doing in the store all that time? He was so astonished when she finally emerged and walked slowly toward him, smiling and dragging her injured feet on the sidewalk as if nothing had happened (by this point her heels were hanging off the edge of the shoes and the Band-Aids were tattered and almost completely falling off), linked her arm with his and said: "Let's go see *Harry Potter*."

And he bought the black patent leather shoes. In the end. He bought them. Went back the next morning to that disgusting shop, bought them without trying them on, and went straight home with the box. "There's probably a special section of hell for idiots like me," he told her when they sat on the balcony drinking coffee, the empty shoe box between them and the black shoes on his feet. Margie leaned over to the shoes, polished them with the hem of her skirt and held them up to her face, straining to see her nose reflected in the lacquer. "Stop rehashing it, Matti. You just wanted to make me happy, what's the big deal?" she said.

Matti looked at the door mistrustfully, wanting to knock again, but his hand remained suspended in midair for a while. From the living room or the kitchen he heard Nadia's voice, high-pitched and almost screechy, lying on the phone: "No, no, Margie's fine. Fine. She's a little bit under the weather. Yes, I gave her an aspirin. She's laying down, yes, I told her to lay down awhile, so she'll get her strength back this evening."

His stomach started murmuring, contracting and dizzying in ominous swirls, and he abandoned the door and ran to the toilet. There, with his thighs on the seat that felt cool and calming, he found himself preoccupied by counting the blue porcelain tiles on the wall over the bathtub. He got mixed up and started over again, wondering if he should begin with the row of tiles at his eye level or at the top row, where the shower head protruded. As he voided himself and simultaneously counted and recounted the tiles, there began to arise in his mind, level upon level, a structure that was both paralyzed and paralyzing, which he called "the practical aspect of the situation," or rather the long and bothersome line that represented its various embodiments: first, his parents, then the wedding hall that had been booked and the wedding hall's owner, the large financial deposit his parents had given the owner, the hundreds of guests who couldn't possibly be notified of the wedding's cancelation, the photographer they had paid in advance, the band, the bed-and-breakfast that had been reserved in the Galilee for that night, the decorated car (not his, a friend from work's), and various other tedious details that branched out from these. For some reason, the image now branded in his mind (he zipped up his pants and buckled his belt) was of Gramsy, and it popped out and rose up insistently from the crowded mass of anxieties and tasks. Her radiant yet absent face (an absence that, strangely, was extremely full and not at all a void), the fold at the bottom of her chin that touched the collar of her festive white dress, which sat quietly in its place, wondrously and innocently unknowing, and which almost brought tears to Matti's eyes at this moment.

He went back to the shut door, infused with a surprising energy derived from the memory of that white collar, and knocked firmly. "Margie!" he called. He waited a moment and added a note of charm to his voice: "Honey? Answer me. Say something." He heard a rustle in the room, from behind the door, or at least he thought he did. There was a sound that resembled padding feet, followed by silence. "Margie," he tried again, fixing his look on the door's smooth brown veneer, but he could feel the desire and the capacity to produce words dying inside him, rotting right in front of his eyes with astounding speed, like summer fruit in a bowl. He looked away from the door and his eyes wandered down the dark hallway to his right, finally settling on a framed tapestry of three roses embroidered in faded red that hung on the wall. "Is this because of what happened last night, Margie? That we fought yesterday? But we made up in the end, that's what I can't understand. When I left you at night we made up and everything was okay and you walked me to the car and then you ran and woke up Yaron to get his cables 'cause my car wouldn't start, so what happened? What happened since then? Would you please come out of there and tell me what exactly I'm supposed to do now? Margie! Do you hear me? Do you want this to end up with a locksmith? Do we have to get a locksmith here to break open the door? Is it going to end up with a locksmith? I demand that you come out now and tell me to my face what you want to say! To my face. I have a right to know, do you hear me? It's my right to at least hear it from you. Can you even imagine what I'm feeling right now? Do you even care what I'm going through with this whole mess you've made?" He spun around and leaned his back against the door, his knees slightly bent from weakness. "I'm thinking over what happened and I can't understand it," he went on. "I can't. Not that I understood your reaction yesterday, but by the end of it I didn't care that I couldn't understand, because we made up. But could you maybe explain to me what that fight was about? What were we fighting about? You sat there for two hours without saying anything. Two hours. With a face like someone died or was sick or something. Until you finally said something. I didn't get it and I don't get it now either, how someone can go off the deep end like that, but at least you said something. And what was that all about—what? Margie, do you hear me? If I told someone what that whole thing was about they wouldn't believe me, I swear they wouldn't; I don't believe it either when I tell it to myself. What would I say? That my girlfriend, the girl I was going to marry the next day, drove herself and me crazy because while we were watching a movie on TV about Leah Goldberg, I said it was too bad I never knew her or met her, and that maybe I would have loved her for real and been able to rescue her from that difficult life she had with men who didn't love her? That's all I said! Margie, she's dead! Leah Goldberg's been dead for years already! Do you get that? How can you throw a jealous fit over a poet who's been dead for years, and not just that but also tell me we're not right for each other and we have to call the whole thing off? Margie!" He turned to the door again and pounded on it with his fists. "Listen to me carefully now, because I'm only going to say this once. If you don't come out now, right now, and talk to me, then I'm the one who doesn't want to get married, not you. Understand? I don't want to marry you—not now, not ever." He stopped speaking, suddenly stunned by the total silence on the other side of the door. A frightened pallor washed over him all at once, galloped up from his feet to his forehead as though a solution had been injected into him. "Margie, are you okay? Just tell me you're okay, Margie. Are you?" He leaned down to his right shin and scratched it hard, as if something had stung him. He pulled his pant leg up to his knee, exposing a red, stinging rash on his skin, and kept scratching, digging his nails in until it was covered with dark red lines.

The doorbell rang for a long time (it sounded like the airport melody: final boarding call) and Nadia froze in the kitchen (gripping a greasy frying pan covered with dishwashing soap), tensing up as if the caller were a collection agency or the security services. Then she snapped out of it, stepped away from the sink, picked up her lipstick from the table and hastily applied it, and smacked her lips together as she walked to the door. Matti's parents walked in, dressed semiformally (the mother's red hair was braided into a high updo studded with pearls, stretching her painted eyebrows out toward her temples, but she wore a zip-up tracksuit top so as not to mess up her hairstyle). They paused just inside for a long time and glanced fearfully around the apartment. Ilan and Gramsy sat side by side on the couch, watching television and snacking on pumpkin seeds. It was Gramsy who cracked the shells in her mouth and carefully placed the shelled seeds in Ilan's hand.

Finally the parents sat down next to each other in the dining area, encircled by several stuffed shopping bags they'd brought with them, which were piled on top of one another like sandbags in a fortification line. Nadia sat down opposite them, poured Coke into tall glasses ("Do you have Diet?" Matti's mother asked), and forbade herself to say anything until they did. She did not trust the volume or tone of her voice. The brief silence—disturbed only by the fizzing of the liquid in the glasses and the loud metallic clangs coming from downstairs, where the gas canisters were being switched out by the gas company workers—sprawled between them, juicy and charged with unspoken ideas. "Okay, so?" said Arieh, Matti's father. He removed his reading glasses from their case, polished them thoroughly, and put them gingerly on his nose. "What's happening, how are things progressing?"

He was an affable man ("Delicate, delicate, a delicate person," Nadia had observed with restrained reverence after their first meeting), at least a head shorter than his wife Peninit (she had changed her name from Penina years ago), clear-eyed, and on his large bald head he had several reddish-purple splotches, covered by a Chicago Bulls cap he wore frequently, winter and summer, much to Peninit's chagrin ("All right, wear a hat, but why a kid's hat? Why? Can't you find something better?"), and even now, when he removed the hat and put it on the dining table, she glared at it resentfully. Two years ago he had retired from his job with the Israel Electric Corporation and now spent most of his days on the beach with his other retired friends, busying himself with long phone calls to the lawyers who were representing him in a suit against his brother (who was not invited to the wedding) over a challenge to his late mother's will.

If it were up to him ("If this were up to me," he often started to say, staring at Peninit, and his voice seeped into the silent loop left by his unfinished sentence), he would have given up the legal battle long ago, negotiated with his brother and reached a compromise. But Peninit, as well as the brother's two sons, viewed any attempt at compromise as a stinging insult and a grave injury to their honor ("It has nothing to do with money"). Things became especially fraught when, shortly after the mother's death, Matti and Margie moved into her home and were kicked out in the middle of the night by Arieh's brother's sons, who claimed the couple had neglected the garden and the lawn, hadn't paid the bills, and had allowed the apartment to deteriorate into such a disgraceful state that the neighbors complained to the sanitation department. Arieh did not believe this slander about his son and his girlfriend, and insisted that the whole affair was "just a mistake, a misunderstanding, as they say," a claim that drove Peninit mad because it attested to what had always tormented and anguished her about Arieh, one single quality that went by three different names: innocence, total blindness when it came to human beings and their motives, and superficial judgment bordering on stupidity.

Now (seated around the brass-framed, rectangular, glass-top dining table in Nadia's apartment, while the tall glasses of Coke sweated beads of condensation) Peninit's adorned fingers, their nails freshly polished in an antique shade of pink, played with a matchbox that sat on the table. She took the matches out of the box, arranged them in front of her in a straight line, then separated them into pairs. She avoided looking at Nadia's face, which had an ashen tone and contained, Peninit sensed, a call for help that Nadia herself was completely unaware of, which was precisely what made it so painful to Peninit.

"I don't know what to say, I really don't," were the words finally blurted out by that ashen face—not by Nadia herself.

Peninit found the courage to look up, although in fact she looked past Nadia, at the milky lamp shade behind her. "What's going on?" she asked. "What's up with Margie?"

The ashen tone vanished, pulled off at once like a rubber mask, and fury mixed with insult imbued Nadia's cheeks with a newfound strength, making them suddenly flower into a purple blush. "Who told you about Margie?" she asked in a metallic voice. "Who's already been blabbing?" They looked at each other awkwardly, momentarily united in their covenant of embarrassment. "We called Ilan. No one answered so we called Ilan, we didn't have any choice," Peninit confessed, uncomfortably rearranging her body on the chair and fiddling with the tracksuit's zipper pull, waiting for things to settle inside her and to find her trusty voice packaged and preserved like a carton of powdered milk. (She was a deputy branch manager at the National Insurance Institute.) "That's not the point now, Nadia, who said and who didn't say. Not the point. Don't even get into that. What's going on with Margie, that's the point," she accentuated and let out the last two words as though spitting out two plum pits she'd been rolling around in her mouth. Nadia stared distractedly into space, touched her chin, and probed around with her fingers for the three tough hairs that had recently sprouted on it. "That Ilan," she said ponderously, almost serenely, "I'll dig his eyes out one day with a teaspoon, that Ilan."

"Did you want me?" Ilan suddenly appeared, as though having erupted from the large air-conditioning unit to the right of the table, along with the chilled air. "What's up?" He went over to the sink and emptied out a dish of pumpkin seed shells.

"Did you tell them about Margie? You open your big mouth?" Nadia fumed. (The couple trembled slightly when she said "them," and turned their synchronized facial expressions toward the front door.) "They asked," Ilan explained, leaning over the kitchen sink with his back to Nadia. "They called, so I told them." Nadia hurried over to him (her thighs got a little tangled up in the dress's satin slip) and pinched his thin arm, hard. "Hurt? Hurt? That's what you did to me, you made it hurt. That's not even anything compared to the hurt you gave me," she cried. Ilan barely forced out a smile, exposing two large front teeth (he was considering getting them filed down) and rubbed his aching arm: "Way to go! Good for you, Aunt Nadia," he said. Arieh started to get up, pushed his Bulls hat away a little, and the glass of Coke fell over and spilled. "Come on, come on, really. We're family. Family," he said, and mopped up the brown puddle of Coke with paper napkins that promptly became sopping wet and disintegrated. Arieh helplessly crushed the napkins between his fingers, and as he did so he noticed a large wet stain on the front of his pants, tried to wipe it off with the crumpled ball of wet napkins, and urged them again, "Family, we are. Family."

Peninit hurried to the kitchen cabinets and examined the marble countertop. "Do you have those reusable paper towels? There's nothing better for these little accidents," she announced, opening and shutting doors. "Reusable?" Nadia sounded incredulous. "You mean, like, a paper towel you can reuse?" She gazed hypnotically at the woman ("She's not my daughter-in-law, or my mother-in-law, that's what she is for Margie . . . But what's the name for what she is to me? I can't remember . . .") with the tower of red hair that now tilted to one side, and the flattened, bejeweled fingers, who was bustling around her kitchen, doing things, saying things, overturning, arranging, detaching, rattling the hanging pots, the long ladle and forks, all with intolerable alertness, an energy and vitality that were out of place and which were an affront, in Nadia's opinion, not only to good taste but to morality itself. A wave of aversion, if not actual hatred, passed through Nadia toward her ("Peninit, Peninit," she remembered, "her name is Peninit!") and every movement she made in the kitchen, exuding her dense vapors of scent ("It's her perfume that makes me nauseous," Nadia remembered), every gesture or tone of voice aroused in Nadia a sharp pain and distress, just like a pair of crude, clumsy hands touching a sick, fragile body lying helplessly in bed. This glacier of loathing swelled and expanded inside her until her throat closed up and she was overcome with shortness of breath (she coughed, trying to alleviate it), provoking terrible fear for her own well-being ("I'm having some kind of heart attack") and of herself ("I could right this minute strangle her with my own two hands, right this minute"). She dug her fingernails deep into her thighs, near her buttocks, trying ostensibly to halt the surging of that glacier, which was now turning into a careening truck threatening to run over and annihilate her and her home ("The home," she remembered with dread: "The home."). She strained her eyes, tried as hard as she could to push away the violent fog and focus on the tall woman ("Peninit, Peninit"), her eyes latching on to Peninit's long earrings with their diamond teardrops that dangled down to her neck, acquiescing to the pleas that finally started cohering inside her ("She could destroy me, that woman. She could destroy the lot of us after all the money she put down at that catering hall. Where are we going to come up with that money if she asks? And she will. She wasn't born yesterday, she'll ask, and where'll we come up with it?"), joining together and slowly rising into a voice, weak at first but then firm.

Nadia found herself walking over to Peninit and putting her clammy hand on her cheek. "You look so beautiful, it's stunning the way you look with your hair up," she said, flustered by herself and by all the tribulations of the invisible path she'd been down these last three minutes. To her surprise, she was completely present in the words she said, and she looked with absolutely genuine marvel, almost admiration, at Peninit's plump, reddish mountain of hair (her own hair had thinned and shed in the past few years, and she tried to reinvigorate it with expensive products and disguise its sparseness with devious hairstyles), underneath which lay her glorious, white forehead. Peninit hugged her, pressed her to her chest, still holding two wet rags (the metal zipper on her tracksuit poked Nadia's eye, since she was far shorter than Peninit). "There, there. It'll be okay. You'll see it'll be fine, open up your heart and it'll be fine," Peninit said and walked Nadia back to the dining table, sat her down and sat down next to her. Nadia covered her face with her hands, then suddenly leaned over and put her lips on the back of Peninit's hand. "God bless. I wish only good things for your kind heart," she said.

Ilan looked at the two of them from his post near the cabinet (searching for the cookies Nadia had hidden, mostly from herself, because of the diet). "Fantastic. Maybe you can just marry each other? That'll definitely be a lot more joyful," he said on his way to the living room and bumped into Matti, who was just coming in.

The three of them gave Matti a questioning look. "She's not," he said curtly and poured himself some Coke. "Not what? What's happening?" his mother asked impatiently. "Not talking," he replied, "doesn't want to talk." Arieh and Peninit exchanged an expressionless look, as though handing each other a package whose destination or origin could not be located. "Well," said Arieh finally, "not to worry. So she won't talk. She doesn't have to. The bride does not have to talk, as far as I recall." Matti looked up at the ceiling and shut his eyes for a second. "It's not that, Dad. Never mind. She doesn't want to get married." "Who doesn't?" Peninit asked distractedly, turning red down to her auburn roots. "Who?! Margie. That's who. Who else could not want to get married?" Matti blurted. Arieh put his hand to his hat and ponderously ran his finger over the sharp edge of the visor: "Some people don't want to get married. Why not? It's possible. I didn't want to get married, I think," he said in a dreamy voice.

Peninit gave him a bewildered look, opened her mouth as if to say something, but Nadia beat her to it, jumped up, smoothed down her yellow quiff and then the front of her dress, brushing off imaginary crumbs. "Margie's good, she's a good girl, Margie. She has the best heart, the best, I'm telling you." She scanned the others, lingering on Peninit. "She just doesn't feel well, that's all. She doesn't feel well, poor girl." She fell back into her seat and jumbled the perfect structure of matchsticks that Peninit had arranged on the table.

There was a silence. Peninit began, clearing her throat first. "No one's saying anything bad about Margie, why would we say anything bad about Margie? She's a gem of a girl. Everyone here," she stopped for a moment, darkened her brows at Matti and then went on, "everyone here loves her very much. Very much. It's just that we have to . . ." She stopped again, digging through her purse for the phone that had started ringing, and disappeared with it into the living room.

Matti looked at his father, who sat opposite him, rummaging in the plastic bags in search of his blood pressure monitor, which he carried everywhere, contradicting the explicit orders issued by his doctor, who had warned that frequent measurements of blood pressure could make his condition worse. "Where is it?" Arieh mumbled to himself, emptying the bags onto the floor, "where could I have put it?" He wandered around the table, stepping carefully among little mounds of folded fabric and wrapped boxes. His hooked nose, which pointed forward like a final act of impudence within the compliant field of his face, and mostly his thin, protruding lower lip, aroused in Matti (who watched from the side) a feeling of sorrow and heartache for this man who was apparently his father, and whose life had passed him by while he constantly backed up against walls. Now, too, there seemed to be a wall in whose shadow he could shelter. (Which one? Mattie wondered. Which wall? He piled up the matches scattered across the table and put them back, one by one, into their box.)

"That was the photographer," Peninit said, back from the living room, as she distastefully surveyed the mess of emptied-out bags on the floor. "She couldn't get hold of you. She said you arranged to meet at five for the pictures, in that park where the foreign workers hang out, by the Central Bus Station, didn't you?"

Matti nodded, turning the matchbox over from side to side.

"Have you by any chance seen my blood pressure . . . ?" Arieh asked her. "I've turned everything out and I can't find it. Maybe it's in your purse?"

Peninit did not respond. She glared at Matti. "What's the story with that Levinsky Park with all those Sudanese? You wanted your wedding pictures with the Sudanese?" she asked.

"What Sudanese?" Nadia was having trouble following. "Who's taking pictures of the Sudanese?"

"Not *of* them," Peninit clarified, "*with* them, in that park they go to. For the wedding. With all those Sudanese foreign workers they brought over here, him and Margie wanted to do their wedding pictures, can you believe it?" She went over to her large bag, took out the blood pressure monitor, and threw it in Arieh's lap.

"I think it's a very nice idea to get their pictures there. It's very picturesque with all those blacks in their white clothes, and Margie with the white dress. Very unique," Arieh said, tightening the cuff on his arm, his lips slightly open and stretching into a faint smile, like a baby finally given his bottle.

"How much did you pay them?" Nadia asked suspiciously. "How much did they ask?"

"Who asked, asked what, what are you talking about?" Matti murmured.

Nadia didn't hear him. "How many of them did you pay—five? Even if each one didn't take a lot, that's still something altogether. I'm sure they wouldn't do the pictures out of the kindness of their heart," she said, searching for something. "I really need a cigarette."

Matti put his hands on his stomach, which had started grumbling again. "Listen," he began, then stopped, facing the same dead end again, the same locked and embarrassing door from an hour ago, which had become the dead end inside him, except that now it was adorned with these faces in front of him, which perked up and jumped out and gaped with eyes and mouths like crazy glove puppets, with the crowing and prattling of his mother and father and mother-in-law ("my mother-in-law, my mother-in-law," he kept rolling the words off his tongue), all of them together and each one separately. All that prattling had nothing to do with what was really true, really honest and private, and which resulted entirely from what there had been and what there still was between him and Margie, between Margie and him, which still existed and was still present, despite the locked door and perhaps even more forcefully because of the locked door, behind which Margie had barricaded herself and which oddly magnified what they shared between them, accentuated what glued them to each other, which had virtually no words, not words that he knew, only what she'd said, Margie, once, about six months ago, when they'd decided to get married, mostly because of Nadia and her suffering, and that night, as they sat in the dark car parked outside her house, Margie had said, "It's an endangered species, all of this." And he'd held her slender, frail fingers between his hands and asked, "Who's endangered?" And Margie had smiled, looking at the dark bushes in front of them, or at something else, and she'd said, "Us. You and me."

"Listen," Matti roused himself and began again, "don't interfere. Please get your arms and legs out of our business."

"The boy is right," Arieh concurred, writing down in his little notebook the latest blood pressure reading. "They're fighting, him and Margie, or not fighting, it's none of our business."

"What do you mean, *right*? How can you say he's *right*?" Peninit fumed. She turned to Matti, practically pinning her face onto his ("Her face like that, up close, it must be like what Picasso saw when he painted those strange, dismantled faces," he thought). "What do you mean, none of our business? What? I want to understand. Five hundred people are going to be in that wedding hall in a few hours and there's no bride and no nothing, and it's none of our business? Then what is our business? It's like if we were all sailing along in one boat and you suddenly took a drill out and started drilling a hole in the boat, and then told me it's none of my business! It's just like that," Peninit huffed, rattled by the rhetorical effort. She sat back down in her chair, took a sip from the glass in front of her, and grimaced: "Disgusting. This Coke has gone completely flat."

Ilan came closer and rapped his finger on the table three times. "Hear ye, hear ye!" he exclaimed, imitating some imaginary crier, his eyes aglimmer with a mocking spark. "She moved the vanity and blocked the door."

"Who?" Nadia asked in a panic.

"Margie. That's what she's done. I walked by the room and heard someone dragging something. I'm sure that's what she was doing. She blocked off the door with the vanity," he said.

"But there were things on it. Bottles, lots of things on it. And the picture of Natalie," Nadia said, turning pale.

"Maybe she moved the things off first. She might have done that," Ilan reassured her, alarmed at the impression his news had made.

"I'm not buying that," Matti said, standing up. He went over to the sink and drank straight from the tap ("Why would you do that? There's cold water in the fridge!" Nadia called out), then added, "Not buying it. She locked the door, what does she need to move furniture for?"

They pondered his observation for a long time, looking down at the table, each wondering separately and all of them together (over their heads the low dining room lamp dispersed a pale yellow light that moved in slow circles, so slow that it was hard to perceive its motion with the naked eye, and then settled in above them in the form of a shining dish that brought to mind a cloud of dust or a halo) what the meaning of this escalation in the other room was, and whether it had any meaning at all, and whether there really had been an escalation in this paralysis that the bride had imposed upon herself and them. Still, they could not deny the sense that this latest news, however they were to comprehend and interpret it, represented a "step up in the situation," as Arieh finally put it.

"Well," was what he said, unwittingly imitating Ilan by rapping on the table with his fingers, "whether she moved the vanity or didn't move the vanity, it's a step up in the situation, as they say." Then he cleared his throat and added, "We need to call a locksmith to break open the door. That's my opinion."

Peninit gave him a grateful look, stopped herself from expressing her relief too openly, so as not to aggravate the others, and asked fawningly, "Was it all right, your blood pressure reading, Arik'leh?"

Nadia sat silently tugging at the lace sleeve of her dress. Then she seemed to become a little muddled, and said, "We'll wait a bit with the locksmith. Let's wait a bit more, we don't have to get hysterical."

Peninit exclaimed, "Nadia! Nadia! Listen to me. It's not hysterics, this is a truly difficult situation. For all of us. Think about what's happening to Margie, think about her locked up in that room, how she might feel, think of that."

"No one's calling any locksmith to break down any doors," Matti said, his voice extinguished almost to a whisper, so that his parents had to lean over the table to hear him.

"What?" Arieh whispered. "What did he say?"

Peninit's face was rigid. She reached out for the phone, biting her lower lip. "I'm calling the locksmith now, so he can finally open up the door and we'll see what's going on with that bride."

"No," Matti said, "you're not. Everything's always by force with you, always force. You're not going to force Margie out, let me make that clear. I respect" (he stomped his foot a little when he said that word, and his nostrils quivered) "her behavior even though I don't understand it. That is what you are incapable of understanding. That I respect" (he raised his voice) "without understanding."

Peninit threw her head back and emitted a peculiar giggle that sounded like a whimper. "Respect! Understand! Don't understand! How about a little respect and understanding for those who have to suffer and pay the price for your bride deciding at the last minute that she doesn't love you and doesn't want to marry you? How about that, maybe?"

No one moved. Roped inside the circle of their breaths, they looked neither at one another nor at themselves, as though they'd been emptied out like a soft egg from its shell, and left hollow. Even the woman who had said those words and hurled that thing into the middle of the room and now stared, like all the others, at the thing she had hurled, which was much too big for her and for everyone else at that moment, and so forbidden that it seemed to go beyond the personal responsibility of any one person and was perceived as a deed committed by an invisible force that had opened up and shattered the ceiling above their heads and cast into the room the giant carcass of an unidentified animal encrusted with blood.

As if in a dream, Nadia began collecting the glasses from the table (avoiding the carcass, she walked around it), holding two in each hand so that the glass clanged (it was mostly she who heard the clanging), placed them in the sink and looked around, wondering, trying to remember what she was supposed to do now, while that drum deep inside her head ("Pay, pay") kept beating ("She said 'Pay,' Peninit did."), continued to rhythmically accompany her every thought, feeling and act ("something about the ones who have to pay") and she felt it might go on beating forever. Like a marionette with its strings cut off by the puppeteer, Nadia was thrown, or rather hurled, from mother to son and back, one moment casting a pleading look at Peninit and begging, "Family, we're family," and the next moment grasping Matti's elbow (his sleeve was wet from the water he'd drunk at the sink) and insisting over and over again, "She loves you, Margie does. Of course she loves you, she does."

Peninit held her arms straight out and walked toward Matti as if she had suddenly gone blind (she really was half-blind, because of her heavy, damp eyelids) and hugged his waist, trying to encompass his rigid body, putting her cheek up against his chest. "I'm sorry, I'm sorry, not this way, really not, I didn't want it this way," she practically sobbed into her son's shirt (he felt her warm, damp breath on his skin, through the fabric, and swore he would not move until it passed—just let it pass), then was suddenly overcome by a sneezing fit that lasted several minutes. She wiped her eyes and runny nose and explained dismissively, "It's my allergies again."

"It's okay, it's okay," Matti said, extricating himself with virtuosic tenderness from his mother's embrace (an intricate act of loosening her fingers on his waist, one after the other, and taking tiny steps backward and sideways, toward the window), exited the kitchen, walked through the living room (Gramsy and Ilan had fallen asleep next to each other on the cognac-colored couch in front of the blaring television, she sitting with her mouth open, head drooped to one side, he curled up with his head on her lap on the imitation leather) on his way to the hallway that led to the bedroom.

Matti looked at the shadowy hallway: the door was still there. It was. His hand reached out and slid over it, stroking, up and down in a caress, smoothing down the sides, then finally gripped the chrome-plated plastic handle. The thick brown color of the door and the deep silence that stood there (Was she asleep? he wondered. Maybe she was asleep) trickled through the pores of his body, seeped inside, and seemed to recharge and colorize his blood cycle, creating a new weather pattern in his entire being. It was not his despair that had changed (he told himself) but the weather of the despair. He put his forehead against the door. Strangely, but not unpleasantly, he felt he had come home. This was home: the locked door, behind which was Margie (Margalit, he remembered. Her name was Margalit). There was a gradual dissipation of the fog inside him, the fog of insult, the violence and astonishment that his mother's words had aroused. The toxic color in her words and her tone ("Toxic," he repeated to himself, as though memorizing something, "Toxic, toxic") had also vanished almost completely, and now a certain transparency arose, a fascinating lucidity of water, at which he dared to look and into which he wanted to gaze so that he could find his own reflection, or Margie's reflection, or both of their reflections together (he could not decide): Margie didn't love him. Maybe. Maybe she didn't love him.

He collapsed onto the floor and sat there with his back to the door, resting his cheek on his knees, which were folded into his chest, and suddenly he seemed small, very small, like a boy who'd lost his key and was waiting in the stairwell for his mother to come home from work. He went back to his thoughts, making progress ("I'm making progress," he told himself), appearing in his mind's eye as that knight who thrashes his sword through the thicket of trees and bushes and cuts away a path for himself. How had he not thought of that? How had he not even considered that possibility, the worst of them all ("And not an unlikely one," he reproached himself), during the hours in which Margie had locked herself in the room and said she wasn't getting married? How?! The complaining voice inside him abruptly quieted down and a different one flickered, then broke through: of course the possibility had not occurred to him. Of course it hadn't. Because she'd said she wasn't getting married, not that she didn't love him. Not getting married. And since when was "not getting married" synonymous with "not in love"? Matti made fists with his hands and listened to the grating of a

third voice, a stubborn and diligent and extremely monotonous one, which drowned out the previous ones: but she's
the one who wanted to get married in the first place. Not
him. She wanted to get married. Margie. Because of Nadia,
she wanted to. She did want to. He rubbed his eyes hard,
until they stung. Through the stinging, he tried as hard as
he could to conjure up Margie's image before his eyes (he'd
suddenly forgotten what she looked like) and project it onto
his eyelids: Margie rinsing out her mouth with mouthwash,
spitting out the strong green liquid too loudly, proud of herself and full of self-pity ("This stuff is horrific."); Margie putting together a TV stand from Ikea, losing two screws and
finding them under the fridge (how they'd fought at first
over deciphering the assembly instructions, and how they'd
laughed when they dragged the fridge out and its wheels
broke); Margie opening the front door for him, standing
there with tears streaming down her face (he never imagined
anyone could have so many tears) after she'd finished reading the last page of Chekhov's biography ("He died, Matti.
Chekhov died," she informed him through her tears); Margie
munching crackers in bed, scattering crumbs on the sheet;
Margie gravely explaining, as she polished her toenails, that
they had to do the wedding pictures (at least part of them, if
not all) with "those poor Africans, the foreign workers" ("If
we're going to get married, Matti, we have to share our joy
with the most unfortunate ones, you understand? Otherwise

it won't be real joy"); Margie falling silent for long hours, becoming air, turning ashen (everything turning ashen: her olive skin; her greenish-brown eyes that got duller and duller as though someone had covered the pupils with thimbles; her dark hair tied sloppily at the back of her neck, with a few gray flyaways that seemed to reproduce themselves in a geometric sequence under the light of the reading lamp; her gnawed fingernails); Margie sitting cross-legged on the concrete railing in the university courtyard the first time he met her, wearing a blue-and-white checkered dress buttoned up to the neck ("the orphanage dress," he called it), smoking half a cigarette and tossing it, lighting another, praising him excessively (he thought at the time) and perhaps artificially (he suspected at the time) for his choice of majors (philosophy and political science) and saying, "I'm not talented with ideas, unfortunately. All those ideas fall apart on me when I cook them, like a curdled sauce." Margie naked.

Weariness spread through Matti's body. With his head on his knees, on the threshold between sleep and wakefulness, voices reached his ears from the kitchen and the living room (the apartment was small, yet it seemed as if entire expanses separated him from them), the doorbell played its stupid (he thought) melody a few times, and everybody's cell phones rang in succession and, at one point, concurrently.

He was amazed by the tranquility, by this cradled, placid feeling he was immersed in, like a warm bath, surprised (he smiled to himself, a thin smile with his head still buried in his knees) at how sweet this sensation of having defected from the battlefield could be. And he had defected, at this moment, in both body and mind, hardly bothering to look out from a distance at what he had abandoned, entirely devoted to a new and completely different expanse that had opened up inside him, with different enquiries. Did he love Margie? Really love Margie? Really love who she was, she herself, as distinct from him? Did he really love her for herself and not for him?

(What is "really"? Is anything "really"? he wondered.) He suddenly knew, in a way that could almost not be articulated or justified, that what Margie had done, what she had declared ("Not getting married") had stemmed not from a process of consideration ("Consideration," he dismissed) and reaching conclusions, but rather from within some sort of musical change, a new melodic entry into herself. He perked up his head. Ilan's rolling laughter reached him from the living room. "What did you say, Gramsy? What's that word you just said?"

Without getting up (now leaning slightly to one side), he banged on the bottom of the door with his hand. "Margie!" he called out in a low voice, looking at the corner of the hallway, at the spot where the walls met the molding. "I'm not going to bug you anymore, Margie, you need to know that. I don't understand why you're doing what you're doing, and now I think I'm not going to get back at you for it. Not ever. I'm saying this honestly. Now I think I don't feel like getting even with you, and not because I pity you. Understand this: it's not from pity. I don't know if you're ever coming out of that room or not." He paused for a moment, considered, then went on. "I don't know what you're planning, or if you even know what you're planning to do. There's major chaos here, you must understand that. Major." (He lay flat on the floor and tried to peer through the gap under the door, surprised at how little light came through. "Maybe Ilan was right and she did block the door with the vanity," he mused). "But now the only thing I . . . " He sat up again and stopped, squinting, "The only thing I ask is for you to just tell me if all this happened because you understood, or you told yourself, or something, that you just don't love me. That's what I want to know, and I think I deserve to know." He stood up, brushed off his pants and went to the bathroom. He turned the faucet on, washed his face a few times, and looked at his wet and enigmatic face in the mirror above the sink ("I have no opinion about my face, no opinion," he thought), still holding his hands under the flow of water.

When he came out, Matti walked down the hallway and gave another glance at the brown door, and his gaze fell on something on the floor: a large piece of paper torn from a notebook. He quickly picked it up and looked at it. Margie. Margie's handwriting in short lines. Matti's hands trembled slightly and he shook them, to calm the tremor, went back into the bathroom, sat down on the toilet bowl with the lid down and read.

The Prodigal Daughter

On her journey, the stone said to her:
How heavy your steps have become.
Will you—the stone then asked her—
Reach your forgotten home?

On her journey, the shrub said to her:
Your stature is no longer tall.

How—the shrub then asked her—
Will you go, if you stumble and fall?

The milestones could not be sure
If the stranger was master or damsel,
And the milestones did rise tall,
Prickling and piercing like brambles.

On her journey, the well called out to her:
How thirsty your lips are, how dry!
And she knelt down and drank the water
And slowly began to cry.

He folded the paper and put it in his shirt pocket and walked through the living room to the kitchen. (Ilan and Gramsy were no longer on the couch, having joined the others, leaving the couch cushions in disarray like two teenagers on summer break.)

"You've finally come!" his mother rejoiced. "Sit down, listen to this." Matti scanned the room with surprise: something had changed in the past half hour, while he'd been gone, as though stagehands and dressers had visited at intermission in a play and changed the sets and costumes. The air conditioning had stopped working—this was the first hard fact. His father was sprawled on a massage recliner they'd dragged in from the living room because of his backache, and it vibrated beneath him, sending shudders through his upper body, which was clad in nothing but an undershirt. The others were also in various stages of disrobing, and looked not unlike a family gathered for a cookout on a traffic island on Independence Day. In place of a barbeque a floor fan had been positioned in the middle of the dining area (although the nook known as the dining area did not really have a middle, having been sliced out of the kitchen, living room, and hallway together). He looked right and exhaled, looked left and exhaled, and went back to the middle. His mother had taken off her tracksuit top and was wearing a bright fuchsia stretchy tank top that hiked up and exposed her midriff. Nadia had removed the formal dress she'd bought for the wedding (Matti's heart sunk) and had on a cotton robe with large pockets, in which her hands constantly burrowed. Gramsy had been extricated from the formal white-collared dress and put into a thin hand-knit sweater, while Ilan had taken advantage of the climate (Matti suspected derisively) to change into a tight mini-tank top that provided no coverage for his nipples or navel. Around his head was a turquoise sash that he'd tied on the side (taken from Nadia's robe).

Matti sat down at the dining table next to Peninit (he still wore his long-sleeved shirt, and swore he would not unfasten so much as a single button, to distinguish himself from them), who held his hand and explained: "Are you listening? There may be a solution. I talked to Sophie, remember her? From my work?" (Matti took deep breaths, praying the preamble would not become too detailed). "So?" he said. "Well, Sophie told me they have special psychologists" (she accentuated the word *special* with both her voice and her lips) "for these situations. Special ones, who know how to handle special situations, see?" "So?" he repeated, pulling his hand back, "So what?" "So we looked on the Internet, me and Dad, and we found this office, we found one!" Her voice climbed up and her eyes sparkled ("I never noticed what beautiful eyes she actually has," Matti realized). "*You* found it," Arieh corrected her from his seat. "It's called 'Regretful Brides,'" Peninit went on, "and they work 24/7, they come especially for emergencies with brides. I mean . . . You know what I mean." She stopped suddenly, afraid to get into any more trouble with her son. Matti gave her a bored look. "That's not by force, having a psychiatrist come talk with Margie and convince her, is it? That's convincing, not forcing. Isn't that right, that it's not called forcing Margie out, Mattileh?" his mother pleaded, eagerly monitoring every stir in his facial muscles.

"She really doesn't feel well, the poor girl. Margie doesn't feel well," Nadia's voice piped up, making its contribution. (She'd made a decision, and was doing her best to stick to it, that she would soften and smooth over the emergency relationship with Peninit as much as she could, so that Peninit wouldn't turn against her and bring up the issue she so feared. This strategy contradicted her nature and was utterly exhausting, and at times she felt as though a huge tray, loaded with glasses, were resting on her head while she tried to balance on a thin rope stretched over an abyss.) "Maybe this doctor can give her a pill to calm her or something. Maybe she's stressed out, the girl, and she needs a pill," Nadia added.

Matti drummed his fingers on the table and said nothing. "So we asked her to come," Peninit plucked up her courage and confessed. "We asked the psychologist and she'll be here soon. Dr. Julia, that's her name." "Julia is her first name,"

Arieh intervened, "not her last name. You should have asked for her last name." Peninit gave him a withering look: "Stop. At least don't get in the way."

With some effort, Matti asked, "So she's coming?" (In fact he was drowning in his own contemplations: "The prodigal daughter. The prodigal daughter. Why was she bringing up the prodigal daughter? And besides, wasn't the original called 'The Prodigal Son'?" He strained his memory, reading a headline that flickered for an instant on the screen of his consciousness, then turned off, then flickered back on: "Song of the Prodigal Son." He spluttered on a sudden shortness of breath that rattled him and then passed, leaving him depleted and limp.)

His mother's voice roused him: "She's coming, this psychiatrist. We'll send Ilan out to wait for her in a minute, so she doesn't get lost in these buildings. She takes two thousand for a home call."

"It's on me!" came Gramsy's voice all of a sudden, to everyone's astonishment. "The doctor's on me." She gripped her wallet tightly in her lap.

"Does she get what's going on? I thought she wasn't getting it," Peninit whispered to Nadia, who blew her nose loudly and shook her head in disbelief. "That's her whole monthly stipend. Most of it, anyway," she said.

Peninit bit her lips, considered for a moment, then went over to Gramsy. "Gramssy," she called out loud, mispronouncing the *s*, "Gramssy, you don't have to pay. There's no need. We'll be fine. What's a doctor's fee compared to all the expenses we've had? You hold on to your money, Gramssy." She looked around to gauge the impression her gesture had made, then sat back down.

"Well," said Matti (so embarrassed by his mother that he'd buried his face in his hands). "Well," he repeated, slowly taking the folded paper out of his pocket and spreading it out before him, "there's something from Margie."

"What? What?" Everyone grew very excited and huddled around him, apart from Gramsy, who kept sitting on the straight-backed chair, still clutching her wallet and running her long lizard tongue back and forth over her dry lips.

"Why didn't you say? What were you waiting for?" Peninit grumbled, glancing at the page. "Did she write that to you?"

Matti hesitated. "I don't know. I think Leah Goldberg wrote it," he said eventually.

"Who?" asked a puzzled Nadia, snatching the paper out of his hand. "Who's Leah Goldenberg?"

"Goldberg, not Goldenberg," Arich corrected her and looked at the piece of paper now held by Nadia. "It's a poem," he added in a disappointed tone.

Nadia stared at the page. "How can you say someone called Leah Goldenberger wrote this? It's Margie's handwriting. I know it is. This is Margie, not some Leah Goldenberg."

"Goldberg, Goldberg," Peninit corrected her. "She's a poet. She was on the radio. Didn't you hear Leah Goldberg on the radio?"

"Goldenberg, Goldberger, Goldberg, Goldenberger—those names of theirs will be the death of us," Ilan mumbled desperately, taking hold of his bushy eyebrows between his thumbs and fingers and tugging at them.

Nadia tried to read what was written on the piece of paper, but her eyes glazed over. "Margie wrote this. Dear soul. She wrote a poem." She held it out for Matti. "Here. You read it to us."

Matti looked at the truncated lines, written in Margie's incredibly round and fluent handwriting. He choked up a little, cleared his throat, and quickly blurted: "Song of the Prodigal Daughter."

"Oh, but she wasn't prodigal, not Margie," Arieh interrupted, sounding thoughtful, as he fanned his face with a dustpan. "She worked hard, from age fourteen, and she never wasted a penny. She told me all about it. Not like these spoiled kids today, who get everything handed to them on a silver spoon." He gave Matti a reproachful look. "Today children are prodigal, throwing money around right and left, but not Margie. I'm really impressed by her."

"Dad, I don't think you know what the word means here. It's from the New Testament, there's a story called 'The Prodigal Son.' This one is about a daughter who gets lost, but then she comes home. It's not about being wasteful," Matti said drily. (From the corner of his eye he glanced at Nadia, at Gramsy, and back at Nadia, at their similarly ossified expressions, which understood nothing yet comprehended everything. He tried to ignore the elevator loaded with dark distress climbing up inside him, from the pit of his stomach to his neck.)

They lowered their eyes, or at least so it seemed to Matti, even though he didn't look up from the page, and his father's voice reached him from a distance, sounding dulled, as if it were coming through a shut window. "Well, the prodigal daughter is something else, like you said. That's pretty, what she wrote. 'The Prodigal Daughter' instead of 'The Prodigal Son.' I get it."

Nadia stood up straight and tensed all her muscles, as though her body were tied to a pole with rope. "Natalie," she said in a foreign voice, "she made that poem about Natalie, Margie did." Then she paused before adding: "She got lost, Natalie. The girl got lost, just like the poem says." With extraordinary gentleness, as if in a dream, she pushed Ilan, who moistened his fingers with water and smoothed them over her face to cool her.

The doorbell played its unflagging tune, not stopping even when the door was finally opened. The unfamiliar woman who entered had to repeat herself twice, loudly: "Regretful Brides. I'm the psychologist you called from 'Regretful Brides.'"

Nadia fled to the bathroom to wash her face and apply blush, while Peninit walked the doctor to the dining table, then changed her mind and led her to the living room. Arieh, Matti (who dragged the recliner back to the living room for Arieh), and Ilan, who linked his arm with Gramsy's and helped her along, hurried after them. The doctor sat down on the couch with her legs close together, clad in shiny nylons, and placed a large binder on her lap. "Where is the bride?" she asked in a hoarse, stern voice that confused Peninit a little ("So young and already a doctor!" she marveled). "Oh, she's not here. Not here," Peninit replied. "Then where is she?" the doctor insisted, and Matti answered instead of his mother: "Margie" (somewhat irritated by all the "shes" being thrown around, he wanted to demonstratively say her name) "has been locked in the bedroom since around midday. She won't open the door and won't talk to anyone. That's more or less the situation."

"Margie?" the doctor wondered. "What sort of name is Margie? Are you from South Africa? I was just with a South African family. Cape Town."

"Margalit," Matti explained, "Margie is short for Margalit."

The doctor surveyed him ("from head to toe," he thought, "she has no shame, this woman") and asked, "Are you her brother or the one who's marrying her?"

Matti gave her a crooked stare (his face went slightly lopsided) full of bewilderment, felt himself swirl around in something, as though his foot had sunk through a thin membrane over a gushing flow of water, which pulled him down dizzily into a whirlpool of darkness, and the words "I'm her brother" tickled the tip of his tongue.

Peninit said: "He's the groom. He's my son and he's the groom."

The doctor furrowed her brow and wrote something down in her binder. "Where are the parents?" she asked without looking up.

"Here," Peninit said, pointing to Arieh, who was shuddering in his recliner, kneecaps jumping. "Him and me, we're the parents."

A thinly ironic smile came over the doctor's face. "The bride's parents, I meant. The one who's shut in her room."

"Margie's father died five years ago and the mother will be right in," Matti said, glancing at the living room doorway. "Where's she disappeared, now that we need her, that Nadia?" Peninit whispered hotly in his ear.

Nadia walked in, freshly made up, though her eyebrows were penciled on slightly crooked: one was lower than the other. She shook the doctor's hand for a long time, then kept holding it between her two hands. "Margie is sad. She has a lot of sadness in her heart, that girl," she explained, looking straight at the doctor. "Write that down," she implored her, looking at the open binder on the doctor's knees. But the doctor stopped writing, pulled her short skirt farther out over her knees, and asked, "Why do you think she's sad?"

Nadia sat down next to her on the couch, digging through the pockets of her robe again. "I don't know," she said quietly, almost whispering. "What? What was that?" the doctor leaned close. "I don't know, I don't know anything," Nadia murmured. The doctor opened the binder again, looking for the appropriate page. "There are a few routine questions here that I need to ask before I talk to her," she said. "To who?" Arieh asked, puzzled. "To Margie, of course. The bride," she replied. "But she's not talking! That's why we asked you to come here," Arieh said, and then he lowered his voice: "She's not talking to anyone. All she does is write poetry."

"How old is Margie?"

"Twenty-four. She'll be twenty-four next month," Nadia answered.

"Does she live at home?"

"Yes, with me all the time, at home," she said hesitantly (debating whether or not to tell the doctor about the brief period of time during which Margie and Matti had lived in his grandmother's home).

"What does she do? Is she studying? Working?"

"She's a university student. Not at the local college—at Tel Aviv University. And she works, too."

"What is she studying?"

Nadia's eyes glazed over awkwardly for a moment. "To be a teacher. She wants to be a teacher," she said finally.

"Literature and theater," Matti clarified. "But she's switched majors a few times. Before that she was doing history, archeology, art history, and French culture."

The doctor glanced at him. "Are you also a student?" she asked, and he nodded.

"He's graduating soon," Peninit intervened. "With honors."

The doctor flipped a page in the binder. "Brothers or sisters?"

Silence.

She looked up. "Brothers or sisters—does Margie have any?" she repeated, accentuating each word.

"Marmion!" Gramsy's voice suddenly screeched through the silence. *"Marmion!"*

"What is she saying?" the doctor asked. Peninit tried to capture her eyes and mouthed the words: "She's not right. Not right."

Ilan went over to Gramsy, rearranged her sweater sleeve, which was tangled around her arm and snagged on her watch strap. "Stop, Gramsy, that's enough. Why do you keep saying that word? You starting again?"

But Gramsy shoved him away gently and stuck her neck out like a chicken. *"Narmion! Narmion!"* she exclaimed stubbornly, with peculiar fury.

Nadia shrank back in the corner of the couch and wrapped her shoulders in a throw that was lying there. "Margie's the big one. There's Natalie, the little one. Three years younger than Margie. She's gone," she said.

"She passed away?" the doctor asked cautiously.

Nadia shook her head. "No, no, she's alive, poor girl. Natalie's alive. She's gone," she said into the blanket, then held it over her face up to her eyes, like a veil.

The doctor gave Matti a questioning look.

"Ten years ago Natalie left school and disappeared, and they never found her."

"I see," the doctor said slowly, and wrote something down (not from right to left as Hebrew is written, Matti noticed).

"And just imagine this, Dr. Julia . . . " (Peninit began but then paused, having realized that she couldn't remember or didn't know the doctor's last name; then she forged ahead.) "To this day—to this day!" (her voice escalated) "they haven't recognized them" (she jerked her head at Gramsy) "as HDA victims. To this day! And it's impossible that it wasn't HDA, what happened to Natalie. It's impossible. I mean, there's no doubt that it was HDA."

Matti closed his eyes. "Mom!"

"And with all my senior connections at the National Insurance Institute, and I do have them, I couldn't get anything to move. I couldn't get them recognition as an HDA family. Dear God, what could it be other than HDA—what? Was it a flying saucer that came from outer space and kidnapped the girl?" Peninit tugged on the tank top that had climbed up above her naval in her excitement.

"It's not certain that it was HDA. Do you know better than them what's HDA and what isn't HDA?" Arieh argued. "I trust them to know, up there, if something isn't definitely HDA."

Nadia stood up, the blanket fell to the floor, and she left the room.

"I'm sorry, perhaps my Hebrew isn't good enough, but what is HDA?" the doctor asked Matti with some embarrassment.

"It's an abbreviated acronym," Arieh intervened from

his armchair. "Do you know what an acronym is? Hostile Destructive Activity. That's what the acronym means."

"*Narmion!*" Gramsy screamed again hoarsely, slapping her thighs with both hands and rocking back and forth on her chair. "*Marmion!*"

Peninit stared at her for a moment, as her face slowly became lucid then drooped to her chin. "Did I say something wrong?" She looked pleadingly at Matti, then at the doctor. "Was there something wrong with what I said? I was just . . ." The doctor stood up and rearranged a bobby pin in her shimmering bun of hair. "I'll go see about Margie," she said.

Arieh's phone rang. He stared at the number on the screen with a look of dread. He did not answer. "It's Mano Dvir, from the catering hall," he said. "Third time he's calling. Should I answer?" Peninit put both her palms to her temples. "I don't know, I don't know, do whatever you want." The ringing stopped briefly, then started again. "I'm answering," Arieh warned them, "I'm answering his call, just so you know." But Peninit grabbed the phone from him: "Give it to me, I'll answer him." For some reason she quickly slipped her feet into her shoes before speaking. "Yes, Mano. No, there's nothing to worry about. You heard from who? From who? Yes, yes, the bride isn't feeling well, she's a little under the weather, but the doctor's here now. Yes, a doctor. It'll be fine. Yes, of course we know about the deposit." (She glared at Arieh.) "Who said anything about canceling? Why would we cancel? Okay, listen, I'm in the middle here, I'm in the middle. We'll talk afterward. Yes, of course, we'll let you know." She hung up and hugged the telephone to her chest.

"What did he say?" Arieh wrapped the blood pressure monitor's cuff around his arm and squeezed the bulb. "What did he have to say for himself, that thief?"

Peninit collapsed onto the low couch next to Ilan, trying to eavesdrop on the hum of voices coming from the hallway, near the locked door. "Shhh . . . Let me hear."

The doctor was led to the hallway and stood outside the door, clutching the large binder to her chest. "Margie!" she called, waited for a moment, then went on: "Hello, Margie. This is Dr. Julia Englander." ("Answering machine," thought Matti, standing beside her.) "I'd like to talk with you. Would you be willing to talk to me?"

The familiar silence prevailed, except that now Matti was sharing it with someone. Her perfume, reminiscent of citrus and bergamot, reached his nostrils—assailed them. They waited. "How many hours has she been in there, did you say?" the doctor whispered. "Seven, I think. A little over seven," he replied, looking at the doctor's exceptionally thin and birdlike profile, whose outline glowed in the shadowy hallway. "And she hasn't come out to use the bathroom in all that time?" she whispered. "There's an en suite in there. But anyway, she doesn't go the bathroom very often," he realized. "What do you mean?" she questioned him. "That's how she is. She can go for hours, holding it in for hours and hours," he admitted awkwardly. "That's bad for her kidneys," the doctor noted gravely, and he nodded in agreement, perplexed by the strange unfolding of events that had led to him standing outside a locked door in an ugly hallway, debating the state of Margie's kidneys with a stranger.

The doctor interrupted his musings. "Could it be because of the dress?" she asked. "What dress?" Matti wondered, a little dazed. "The bridal gown. Lots of brides break down and get cold feet at the last minute because of the dress. Like if there's family pressure to rent a six thousand shekel dress and they wanted the thirteen thousand one, or the fifteen thousand one, and some girlfriend makes a comment. That sort of thing." He stared at her (lingering on the brown mole next to her nose). "Thirteen thousand?" he said. "Margie is not at all the type you're thinking. Not at all the fifteen thousand type. A friend of hers who's studying design sewed the dress for her as a gift. I don't even have any idea how much it cost, if it cost anything at all." He pulled out his phone and ran his finger across the screen. "Here she is in the dress. She tried it on last night."

The doctor removed her glasses and looked. The bride's straight, dark hair fell in two heavy, desperate cascades on either side of her face, plunging down to her gaunt shoulders, which were covered by the dress's translucent white fabric. A single, muted pearl glimmered at the round neckline. Her large, slightly slanted eyes were too wide open, almost unnaturally so, and blended in the picture with the very dark, very bushy eyebrows, so much so that at times it looked as though the place where her eyes should have been was cut out, with only two dark, round holes testifying to their location. She had her hand held up to her cheek and the dress's wide sleeve drooped down a little, exposing her forearm, revealing five colorful beaded bracelets that reflected dancing light on the wall, and whose cheerful jangling one could almost hear.

"She's pretty," said the doctor, handing him back the phone. "Margie, can you hear me? This is Dr. Julia Englander. You can just answer yes or no, that's fine." They waited quietly again. ("It's pointless, we're pointlessly waiting," Matti thought gloomily, and the thought slid into a corner of his mind, then bounced back to another corner, like a bowling ball in an empty, windowless room.)

From behind the door there came a feeble, strange bleating sound. They looked at each other and tilted their heads. Something bleated again, almost singing, in a mechanical voice that sounded like a baby's whimper, or an imitation of a whimper: "Ye . . . es," and after a moment or two, "No . . . oo."

"Is that Margie's voice?" the doctor asked dubiously. Matti shook his head. "I don't think so. She's never made a sound like that." There was silence for a moment (Mattie secretly placed his thumb on the pulse throbbing in his wrist), then the voice bleated again: "Ye . . . es," and then, "No . . . oo." It sounded wobbly and withering, like a radio with its battery running out. (That's it—the realization struck him—a battery.) "It's a doll," Matti said, "it's not Margie at all, it's a doll. You know, one of those dolls that talk when you turn them over." "Does she have a doll?" the doctor asked curiously. "No, of course not!" he retorted, and his panic turned over and mounted into terrible fury, almost hatred. "Margie!" he pounded on the door and kicked it. "You've had it if you don't open up right now, this minute, and quit all these games, do you hear me? You've had it!"

The doctor looked at him without saying a word, her gaze gleaming from behind her glasses, and went back to the living room.

"I don't think I can be of much help without seeing her. I have to see her," the doctor informed Peninit.

"Then we'll break down the door, there's no choice," said Arieh, avoiding the menacing look on Peninit's face, which passed over him and roamed around in search of Matti.

"Don't look at me. You can take your eyes off me. Do whatever you like, break down the door, don't break it down, I don't care," Matti said and went into the kitchen.

The parents looked at each other helplessly. "We have one hour, tops, to let Mano Dvir know if we're canceling. One hour tops," Arieh said. Peninit went over to the large window, opened the glass door and then the blinds, leaned over the railing with her whole upper body hanging out, and looked down at the street.

"What are you doing?" Arieh hurried over to her, grabbed her arm and pulled her back. "What do you think you're doing?"

"What's the matter with you?" She pushed him toward the recliner, rubbing her arm. "What's got into you? Did you think I was going to jump? Is that what you thought? I needed some fresh air, that's all."

Nadia reappeared. Her coiffed blond bangs were drooping on her forehead, almost covering her eyes. "Did you hear anything from Margie's room?" she asked distractedly. "I thought I heard something. There was something in there, someone crying. It sounded like a baby's voice."

The doctor considered her words. "It was apparently some sort of doll," she said finally.

"A doll..." Nadia echoed. "Which doll was talking?" she wondered, blinking, while Ilan stood behind her, rubbing her neck. "It's okay, Nadia, come on, don't get into that again now. It's okay, Margie just found that doll in there that belonged to..." (he hesitated, articulating her name with some difficulty) "... to Natalie. She just happened to find it there." He took Nadia over to Gramsy, sat her down, and arranged their hands together, clasping each other. "Look after her, Gramsy, the way you know how. Look after her well, this whirling dervish of ours, this sweetheart, so she doesn't go whirling around again and getting into mischief," he urged Gramsy, whose face lit up with her wonderful, inscrutable smile.

"I have an idea of how you can maybe see her," Ilan told the doctor in a purposeful voice.

"How?" asked three voices at once. "How?" They gathered around him (Matti was back from the kitchen), full of expectation, like Boy Scouts about to set off on a night trek.

"We bring one of those ladder vehicles—either a fire truck or a cherry picker, with a ladder that goes up to the third floor," Ilan began self-importantly, but then stopped.

Peninit's face fell. "What are you talking about? A vehicle with a ladder? Well, honestly! It's like we're in kindergarten. A vehicle with a ladder! What about a sandbox—do you want one of those, too?" she dismissed him impatiently.

"He does have a point, actually," Arieh mused. "If we had that sort of ladder on a truck, the doctor could maybe see her through the window. She could just stand there outside the window and talk to Margie."

"Have you lost your minds?" Matti burst out. "Have you gone completely insane? Are you seriously going to listen to this nutcase?" (He waved his hand at Ilan.) "Is Margie some sort of terrorist barricaded in that room, threatening to massacre us all? Next thing you'll be saying the doctor has to dress up as an old Arab lady or something. Good God," he said, wiping his brow.

Without paying any attention to him, Arieh pressed on, growing more and more fond of the idea (and not only because of the benefit it might bring). "I can talk to Avner from the electric company. He has connections with the garage where they keep the trucks with the ladders. I'll find his number in a second." He put his glasses on and leafed through a little notebook.

"Electric company ladders?" Nadia asked with a weak, involuntary smile. (She had retreated, taking no position in the debate over necessary modes of action, and was preventing herself from taking any interest, retiring to a place that was not even her home but a sort of hideout, a secret room that branched off her actual apartment, which in her mind's eye had been impounded by Peninit and Arieh and the polite doctor and even by Matti, and it was all lawful, she thought, it was a lawful impounding, because she sensed what was going to happen on account of the huge debt she owed them for the wedding expenses, and so she quickly retreated, relinquishing what was far more costly than the apartment itself, which was her sense of ownership of the apartment.)

Arieh left the room with his phone, having tried to hush the voices around him with his hand, and came back a few minutes later. "I talked to Avner, I told him the whole story," he announced excitedly. "So here's the deal," he began, and took a deep breath to prepare for his speech.

"Stop it. I don't even want to hear it, I don't want to," Matti said, stomping his foot.

That foot-stomping infuriated Peninit (she once again noticed Matti's black patent leather shoes, which she despised) and at that moment she made up her mind to side with Arieh and Ilan. "Run along," she told Matti impatiently. She picked up her purse, pulled out a coin and put it in his hand: "Here's ten shekels. Go buy yourself a popsicle at the corner store. Calm down. Run along."

Arieh continued: "Avner wants to help, he's a good guy, I know him. But here's the problem: to get an electric company vehicle out here now, he can't do that. He could easily lose his job for that. But he had an idea. He has a good friend, Adnan, from the Palestinian Authority's electrical company, and this Adnan brought one of their vehicles in for repairs at the shop. So Avner says maybe Adnan can come out here with his truck, and it won't be any trouble. No trouble at all. Adnan owes him a favor lots of favors—and he'll do it," he summed up ceremoniously.

"So this Adnan has to get in trouble instead of Avner? That's the solution?" Matti asked caustically.

"Who said he'll get in trouble?" Arieh asked defensively. "Why must you always see the glass half empty? He won't get in trouble. He's used to it, with all their chaos over there, I guarantee you. We don't know what he owes Avner over there."

"Tell him to come quickly," Peninit decreed in a foreboding voice.

One of the doctor's two phones rang (they were on the living room table, in front of her). "Regretful Brides, how can I help you?" she said. She spoke softly for a moment, then hung up. "I don't have a lot of time," she announced. "There's an urgent case with a bride who got out of the car on the way to her wedding. I'll need to get over there."

"She got out of the car just like that?" Arieh asked in amazement, his attention completely distracted from the previous matter. "You mean she jumped out of a moving car on the way to the event hall?"

The doctor shrugged her shoulders. "I'm not sure exactly. But I don't have a lot of time."

Ilan was getting ready to walk out to the parking lot to wait for Adnan's van or pickup truck. ("Is it a van or a pickup?" he asked). He put on Margie's slippers, the woolly ones with squished bunny faces in the front.

"It's a truck, but a small one," Arieh said. "You'll recognize it. And call us right out."

"Does it have any kind of flag on it?" Ilan insisted. "Does it have that flag of theirs, red and . . . blue and yellow, or whatever their colors are?"

"Are you mad?" Arieh sounded horrified. "There will be no flag of theirs here. Over my dead body!"

Peninit went back to the window, leaned over the railing again and looked out, lost in thought. Gramsy and Nadia ate eggplant dip out of the same dish, without a fork, scooping it up with pieces of bread. Peninit watched them sympathetically. "Why don't you both go and lie down? Have a little rest, we'll call you when he gets here," she suggested.

"She'll come out in the end, don't worry. They all come out in the end," the doctor added, as she texted feverishly on her phone.

Peninit looked at her. "What are we going to tell the five hundred guests? Friends from work, neighbors, family— what will we tell them?" The doctor did not answer. It was quiet. They could hear Gramsy chewing and smacking her lips, enjoying the eggplant. Matti lay back in the recliner with his eyes closed (Arieh had gone out with Ilan to wait for the truck), surrendering in exhaustion to a dreamy or nightmarish picture of a different universe, which danced in front of his eyes, rustling and colorful like a bundle of cellophane sheets, a sort of semimute universe. In that space between sleep and wakefulness there were regretful brides who scurried around, tripping over their long veils, skipping past trucks belonging to the Palestinian Authority's power company, and his father walked among them, pleading and urging, with the blood pressure cuff on his arm, which for some reason was covered with shiny, bright green cats' eyes. He woke up with a start, bathed in sweat, and suddenly remembered something. He touched the paper in his shirt pocket, took it out, and unfolded it.

"Again with her poem?" Peninit asked dryly. (Then she thought: "I must update the doctor.") "She sent a poem. Did we tell you Margie sent out a poem she wrote?"

"She didn't write it, Leah Goldberg wrote it and Margie copied it," Matti explained, privately wondering whether "copied" was the correct verb in this case.

"Margie never copied anything. Why are you saying she copied it from Leah again? She was the top of her class," Nadia insisted, suddenly come back to life. She went over to Matti, took the paper out of his hand and brought it to her lips, then held it out to look at the short lines. "Where did Margie get them? All these words?" she wondered.

Matti took the page back and handed it to the doctor. "Read it."

The doctor read silently, furrowing her brow, her lower lip curled into an expression of either bewilderment, misunderstanding, or repulsion. "There's no doubt about it, she's a very special young woman," she said when she was finished.

"Very, very special. Too special, if you ask me. From

morning to night all she does is work on being special, that girl," Peninit commented resentfully. (The fatigue and tension had unbridled her inhibition and sharpened her tongue.)

Paying no attention to her, Nadia went over to the doctor and stood facing her. "What did she say, my daughter?" she asked. "What does her poem mean? Tell me." Just then Ilan flung the front door open and announced: "The ladder's here!" Then he hurried over to Gramsy, took her by the arm, and walked beside her at her measured pace to the front door. "You're taking *her*? Her, too?" Matti exclaimed. Ilan looked surprised: "Why not? She's always with us at family events. You want me to leave her here like a dog?"

They went downstairs, Ilan and Gramsy in the lead, the others behind them.

Matti sat alone in the living room awhile longer. He lay down on the couch, still wearing his shoes, looked at the poem again, folded up the paper and put it in his pocket, and stared at the narrow strip of sky visible through the large window, above the treetops and buildings of the Tel Aviv suburb. He was suddenly filled with awe at this vision of the revelatory sky, and he said to himself: "The skies of Kir'on." A bothersome thought began to adhere, centered around that foolish, unrelenting phrase, "the skies of Kir'on," which, much as he tried to rid himself of and move on to the next thing, nonetheless assailed him again and again, emerging from fragments of other sentences, thoughts and feelings, disrupting them, hindering their proper motion, if they even had any motion, any direction.

With great effort, through this disruption, this "skies of Kir'on" disturbance, he found himself clinging to his earlier question ("What was she trying to say with this poem? What is she saying?"), which now merely aroused boredom and disinterest, as though it were the homework assignment of a lazy student. Still, he tried to animate it and bring it to life, simply because it reminded him of what he knew and recognized as himself, the same self that now seemed extremely ancient, almost prehistoric, impervious to his current being, the one that existed after Margie and Margie's door. He felt as if he'd grown up at once, or grown small at once, in a matter of hours, since the whole business of Margie and her door had begun. He moved the toes of his shoes in front of his eyes while he thought about this, trying to restore his sense of body, to regain a proportionate view of things, and of himself inside the things, which had seemed to have slipped through his fingers, and from that slippage, from the leakage of himself out of himself, from his fear of losing contact with the floor beneath his feet, he could feel the jealousy arising. He was not jealous of Margie, at the thought that she might prefer someone else to him, but he was terribly envious of her. Like her, he longed to lock himself behind a door, to put everything on hold, to rebuff the world and its words, to reduce his entire existence into that space between his breaths and the pillow his head lay on. For a moment he had the urge to go back to the hallway and beg her to open up again, but this time not to make her come out but to make her let him join her, so they could lock the door behind them both.

The phone rang. Arieh told him to come down quickly. On his way out, Matti stopped in the bathroom and then lingered in the dark hallway outside the door. He looked at it quietly, his arms hanging limply at his sides, listening to the silence inside himself, the new silence that hummed its soft melody inside him, as if through a thick blanket, monotonous and circular, reaching the end of the tune and starting over again: "It doesn't matter if she comes out or not, it doesn't matter, doesn't matter, doesn't matter now if she comes out, doesn't matter."

When Matti got to the parking lot he found a sizeable gathering of neighbors and passersby next to a decrepit looking midsized truck with Arabic lettering on its side. The area nearest the building wall and the upstairs bedroom window was occupied by three parked cars, and everyone was discussing how to locate the owners—residents of the building— and persuade them to move their cars.

Adnan, a short, thin young man wearing a red T-shirt that said "Petach Tivka Summer Camps" on the front, had walked away, sat down on the curb, and was smoking a cigarette while he waited. "This is when they come to fix the power?" grumbled a young woman with a stroller. "They'll end up causing a power outage all night with their repairs." Arieh, who stood next to her wearing his baseball cap, aflutter with excitement, did not correct her mistake. ("Don't go opening your mouth and telling everyone about Margie, don't open your mouth," Peninit had warned him earlier.) He scowled at Ilan, who had moved away from the truck and was conversing with someone (Arieh had just instructed him to stand by the truck and hide the Arabic words as best he could). The doctor sat on a nearby wooden bench, next to Gramsy, whose eyes were shaded behind Ilan's gold-framed sunglasses. Gramsy looked around, and every so often she stuck out her long, supple tongue, moistened her lips, and stretched it down to her chin. Matti sat down next to them, assuming the status of a bystander, but a few moments later he changed his mind, walked over to Adnan, and looked down at the young man who still sat on the curb with his feet crossed. "How's it going?" he asked.

Adnan looked at Matti's black patent shoes. "Are you something or other from the municipality?"

"I'm the groom," Matti replied and sat down next to him.

Adnan offered a cigarette. "Total mess, huh?" he said, lighting the cigarette Matti refused and smoking it himself.

Matti looked at the truck. "That elevating ladder—is it going to reach up there?" he wondered.

"It'll reach," Adnan confirmed. "Why wouldn't it? We get it to reach all the way up to the wires. Nothing happens to them, they're all good."

Matti had trouble following. "Who's all good?"

Adnan did not answer. Lost in thought, he tapped the cigarette with his finger, flicking ash on the sidewalk. "Why don't you lock her up?" he finally asked. "Lock her up for two or three weeks, maybe four, let her sit it out."

"Lock who up?"

"Your fiancée. Lock her up," Adnan advised.

"But she's already locked up. How much more locked can I get her?"

"No, no, no," Adnan corrected him, straightening up. "You lock her before she locks herself. Before. After, it's no use anymore." He looked to one side, as did Matti, at a small cluster of neighbors standing around Nadia next to the truck.

"Ten years after the girl left, another one goes," Nadia was saying in a subdued voice, wrapping her fingers around a piece of fabric, a scarf or handkerchief, staring far away above their heads. "I don't have the heart to feel what I'm going through anymore. Where will I get the heart?" she lamented, walking in a circle from one neighbor to the next, touching each one and standing close to them, as if she were circulating among wedding guests.

"And she won't come out? She won't come out of the room?" asked one of the neighbors worriedly. His neck was stabilized in a high orthopedic neck brace. He gave a quick glance at Arieh and then at Matti.

"Won't come out," Nadia confirmed. She looked out beyond them again, at the reddish roof of the shopping center across the street, seemingly broadcasting her voice to something, not someone.

The neighbor in the neck brace held Nadia's clammy hand and stared at the truck. "But why did you bring Arabs to rescue her? Why Arabs? Don't we have our own rescue forces?" he asked. The young woman with the stroller scolded him, distractedly rocking the empty stroller as she held the baby in her arms: "Stop with that. What's it got to do with rescue forces? The bride doesn't want to come out, you heard what she said, she won't come out. What does that have to do with rescue forces?"

Peninit stood there listening bitterly, overcome with an urge to pull Nadia and her words out of there and give them a good shake. ("Be diplomatic," she commanded herself, "diplomatic.") Instead she went over to the circle, made her way to Nadia ("Excuse me, excuse me, I'm sorry") put her arms around her shoulders, gripping tightly, brushed away the hair stuck to her forehead, and led her slowly out of the circle ("She doesn't feel well, she mustn't talk so much," she explained pleasantly) to the bench where Gramsy and the doctor were sitting.

When the parking area near the apartment window was finally cleared, Adnan started the truck up and drove at a crawl to the side of the building (trampling the sparse hedges). Two long, parallel metal tracks, with a small lift attached to them, emerged from the body of the truck and began to extend upward. Adnan got out and opened the side of the lift for the doctor. "Please, Madam," he said with a slight nod.

She hesitantly put one foot, clad in a blue, high-heeled pump, on the metal platform. "Is this thing safe?"

"Of course, don't worry," Adnan promised.

The doctor looked down, pulled her foot back, stood with her legs straight and close together, and bowed her head. "I can't get on it. I have a fear of heights," she whispered to Ilan, who was standing very close on her right side.

"I'll come with you, don't worry. I'll go up with you," he reassured her.

"No, no, that's impossible," she said, shaking her head.

"No one can be with me while I'm talking to her. No one. That's not allowed in a therapeutic situation."

"But I'm no one. I swear, I'm no one. Nobody is more no one than me, and I won't hear a word of what you say, and what I do hear I won't understand anyway, I'm telling you," Ilan insisted eagerly.

She looked wanly at his face, at the turquoise sash tied around his head with a butterfly knot on the side. "All right," she agreed.

They stepped onto the platform. The small lift shuddered, barely rose up from its base, then began climbing slowly to the third-floor window, went straight past it—to everyone's astonishment—and kept going to the fourth floor, where it stopped. Ilan and the doctor were swallowed up behind large, damp sheets that had just been hung out to dry.

"That's not the right window, it's not the right one!" Arieh growled at Adnan. "Where are you taking them—to God Almighty?" Adnan hushed him with a wave of his hand, pressed the left button, and the elevator began to descend again, stopping outside Margie's window.

From afar and below, from the edge of the parking lot where everyone rushed to get a better look (Gramsy was left alone on the bench. A fat, black-and-white stray cat sprawled out next to her, squinting with the heavy weariness of one who's seen it all), the doctor could be seen stretching her arm toward the windowpane, trying to knock on it, unable to reach. She consulted with Ilan and then removed one of her blue pumps, held it out, and used the heel to bang on the window. There was a moment's silence. The high-pitched, slightly squeaky voice of a girl suddenly came from the crowd: "Which of my clothes are new and what's already been washed?"

The doctor rapped on the window with her shoe again. "Let's hope she doesn't break the glass and make people get hurt. That'll be the end of this," Arieh fretted, and was immediately silenced by an elbow from Peninit, who was staring up expectantly. The glass pane slowly rolled along its tracks and the window opened. The bride, with her head behind a transparent veil that plunged to her shoulders and hovered like thick steam around her dark hair, stood at the window wearing dark sunglasses (a glaring sun still blazed from the east). Nadia's hand reached up to her gaping mouth, which sought to unleash an involuntary yelp of joy (she could not remember if she'd ever broken out in a yelp of joy, or whether she even knew how to produce such a sound, which always aroused in her a tinge of discomfort and embarrassment), but she tamped it down with her hand. Margie spoke. With their hands shielding their foreheads against the sun, everyone saw her arms moving while she talked to the doctor for several minutes. She vanished from the window for a moment and then reappeared, holding out a large piece of thick, unrolled paper that filled the rectangular window frame. In the same curly lettering from the poem, the word "Sorry" was written on the paper. The crowd looked up. "What does it say?" Nadia asked, unable to see clearly. "Sorry," said Peninit in a miserable, defeated voice. "She says sorry."

The lift slowly descended, and just then a siren blared in the distance, getting closer and closer. A police car soon stopped by the crowd of onlookers. Adnan noticed it first, and quickly dug through the glove compartment for his ID. "Who's in charge here?" asked one of the two policemen who stepped out and calmly surveyed the crowd.

"Me," Matti felt compelled to say, making his way forward and standing in front of the officers, straightening his shirt collar.

"We got a warning on the phone about a truck with explosives. Where's the truck?"

"There," said Matti and Adnan together, pointing at the truck. "It's the power company, not explosives. There's no explosives," Adnan added, holding out his ID.

Ilan and the doctor stepped off the lift platform and gave the uniformed officers a surprised look. "What did you call the police for? It's all settled with Margie now," Ilan said.

"Settled? What's settled? What did she say?" Arieh demanded.

The policemen walked all the way around the truck, peered inside, closed and opened the bolt on the lift's gate, banged on the sides with their fists a few times, and examined the faded red Arabic letters. "What's that say on the truck?" one of them asked.

"Sorry," said Arieh, who was busy trying to decipher the doctor's frozen expression. "She wrote 'Sorry.'"

The policeman gave him a suspicious look. "What sorry? What are you talking about, sorry?"

Adnan cleared his throat. "This is the electrical company's truck, from the PA. I was just doing these people a favor. It was just a favor I was doing because of the wedding."

The doctor gave him a stern look (Adnan tilted his head to one side, as though trying to dodge a ball kicked powerfully on a soccer field) and furrowed her brow. "This man was doing us a favor," she finally confirmed.

"A favor?! How is this a favor?" Matti snapped. "What did we get out of all this stupid talking with Margie through the window? What do we know now that we didn't know before?"

"Hold on," the officer stopped him, "so now you're saying the guy from the truck in Arabic wasn't doing a favor?"

Matti turned red. "I didn't say that. That's actually not what I said. He personally did do us a favor. He did," he declared, still sounding confused.

Adnan pushed his way forward and stood between Matti and the officer. "Don't listen to him, don't listen, 'cause he's not in charge, he's in charge my foot, 'cause his bride left him on their wedding day—is that a man in charge? He's not in charge, listen to me . . . " He opened his mouth wide and put his face right in front of the policeman's.

The policeman recoiled, squinting. "The two of you are coming to the station with me, right now. With the truck, come with me."

Matti stared at him. A bothersome hum was growing louder, turning into an almost deafening beep in his ears (he covered his right ear with his hand). "I can't start going to stations now," he said with some effort, in a small voice. "Maybe afterward. But now I have a wedding to cancel." He shook his head from side to side, walked away, and sank onto the bench next to Gramsy.

A dusky afternoon light descended abruptly on the parking lot, without anyone noticing, replacing the blazing hot glare from before but leaving the heavy humidity, perhaps even magnifying it (Adnan was led to the truck and one of the policemen sat down next to him in the driver's seat), since it now seemed the asphalt itself were exhaling on them all, dispensing the enormous, densely packed stores of heat it had absorbed all day, breathing them out, not all at once but at a regular, rhythmic pace, steady breath after steady breath, as though unwilling to reveal its entire secret at once, preferring instead to expose it gradually, piece by piece. (The truck engine rattled, groaned, died out, and was restarted. The truck slowly backed out, turned around in the lot, and crawled away behind the police car.) Matti heard Gramsy smacking her lips and wondered what was in her mouth that she was sucking so eagerly. Her total serenity, embodied in her small freckled hands resting on her thighs together, suddenly horrified him, after having merely surprised him only moments before.

"How are you, Gramsy? How's it going?" Matti asked, but she didn't hear him. She kept looking up at Margie's window as if she expected something else to appear there, another sign, or a sign of a sign. (From a distance, near the trampled hedge, Peninit and Nadia were talking with the doctor, who did not look at them but instead bent over and examined a long run in her nylons. Then she straightened up, made her way to the edge of the lot with the two women behind her, got into her car, exchanged a few more words with them through the window, and drove away.)

Matti followed Gramsy's eyes, carried along with them up to the window, his gaze intertwining with hers, which was, he imagined, both vapid and full of expectation, strangely glowing. An old picture surfaced in his memory, of Margie and Gramsy, Gramsy and Margie, on that day, the first time Margie took him to Gramsy's jumbled, yellow apartment.

The old woman was sitting erect in a stiff, straight-backed armchair, wearing a heavy, eggplant-colored knit dress buttoned up to her neck. Her face and eyelids were covered in crude, glowing streaks of makeup (Ilan had done her makeup in honor of the occasion) and her hands clutched each other, and she looked as though she had been marinating herself in this precise position for several hours before their arrival—since morning, in fact. Behind her chair, right above her head, a translucent white curtain billowed, and its hem touched her forehead or hair every so often, but she did not move, did not reach out to brush away the nuisance that apparently did not bother her at all. Margie held his arm, led him to Gramsy's seat (pinching his upper arm lightly as she did so) and said in Hebrew and Arabic, very deliberately, so that Gramsy could read her lips: "This is the one I told you about. What do you think?" Without waiting for an answer, she jumped into Gramsy's lap, wrapped her arms around her neck, and put her cheek on Gramsy's face, near her temple. She shut her eyes. He watched with wonder as Margie sat there in utter delight, with her eyes closed, rocking on Gramsy's lap and rocking Gramsy with her, as though she were a large baby who had to be soothed and put to sleep.

He stood there awkwardly, next to a large bureau, and watched them both. Then he looked away from what seemed to him a demonstrative display of powerful emotions and tenderness, sensing his increasing embarrassment, discomfort and even shame, the kind that arises when one watches a bad theater actor gesticulating, trying with all his heart to animate and magnify the audience's heartfelt emotions. And he was so alarmed. He remembered suddenly how alarmed he felt that day, the internal pallor that colored his awkwardness, that foreign feeling, the alienation from Margie, the evil look she gave him, the look of a hostile witness.

"Hostile," he repeated to himself now, but this time without any alarm, only curiosity and huge wonderment at that sensation, that old coat suddenly removed from the depths of his memory and consciousness to be aired out, spreading an indistinct but unpleasant smell, the smell of closed-up spaces with no daylight. He kept his head turned up to Margie's window but his eyes closed, and pushed away the purring fat cat that nuzzled at his thighs. Actually, there had always been something standing between him and Margie, between him and himself in his relationship with Margie. There had always been something between them, actually. ("Actually, actually," he rolled the word off his tongue, struck by the realization that the minute that word turned up, the downward slope began. The slope always began with "actually.") This thought that occurred to him did not surprise him at all, and it even looked familiar and friendly, so much so that he could surround it with equanimity and confidence, like a boy running all the way around a dodgeball court on his own, without anyone racing him. What was the content of the "actually"? What was its logical, concrete embodiment? What exactly was it that stood between him and Margie, still? He found himself face-to-face with the slippery words that for so long had not wanted to be found and now had been: he always had to bend something inside him with Margie, to constrict, to accept a certain uncomfortable bodily position, and mental position, with regards to her, and to work hard to blur it in his own vision. Always. And it always contained a dirty little secret, a tiny one, a miniscule one, that could not be seen with the naked eye but was there, teeny-tiny, a lie he told himself and her, an "actually" that nestled inside him and bided its time, waiting and waiting. But no longer, he told himself. No longer. For the first time in all those hours that day ("actually, for the first time ever," he thought), a sense of relief ran through him, an enormous release from a burden he had not even been aware of and which had now been lifted, leaving him practically naked, but at the same time with a wild happiness at the nakedness, an almost total relinquishing of secret assets.

He opened his eyes, surprised to discover that Gramsy was still sitting next to him, sailing across her world as if on a pool raft. For some reason he found himself pulling out Margie's note again, spreading it out before him, smoothing out the creases. "Would you like me to read you Margie's poem, Gramsy?" he asked. (He noticed that he'd called it "Margie's poem," but with a wholeheartedness now, which stemmed from the distance, without any pangs of conscience.) She nodded without looking at him.

"On her journey," he began, speaking loudly, examining Gramsy's face. She smiled delightedly and signaled for him to continue.

> On her journey, the stone said to her:
> How heavy your steps have become.
> Will you—the stone then asked her—
> Reach your forgotten home?

On her journey, the shrub said to her:
Your stature is no longer tall.
How—the shrub then asked her—
Will you go, if you stumble and fall?

"Why didn't you say sorry to Margie? You didn't say sorry," Gramsy interrupted. She started rocking back and forth on the bench as though something were bothering her, or as though she were praying.

"What?"

"Sorry to Margie. Why don't you tell Margie sorry?" Gramsy repeated.

"Margie was the one who said sorry," he tried to explain. "Margie wrote 'sorry' on that big paper in the window, remember? She was the one who said it."

The old lady pursed her lips, displeased, refusing any words. "Sorry to Margie," she hissed. Matti opened his mouth wide, about to say something, to flip back what had apparently been flipped over in the old lady's mind, but he stopped and fell silent in dismay. Perhaps Gramsy had read his thoughts before. Perhaps through her withered, diagonal, tortuous instincts, she had guessed at the path he had taken, which was paved with those words that one must not utter and yet one must utter? He examined her face with great attention, with awe. It showed no sign. It remained impenetrable, like a steaming platter covered with a stainless steel cover. "I'll tell Margie sorry, like you say. I'll tell her," he heard himself saying. "When?" the old lady demanded with the impatience of a debt-collector. "Very soon. Soon I'll tell Margie sorry," he promised, amazed at being somehow happy to make her this promise, and even happier to collaborate with her whims.

His mother and father came over to the bench, with Nadia straggling behind them. "We're going to the catering hall, to let the guests know. We'll have to stand up there and tell the guests," said Arieh, crumpling his Chicago Bulls cap in his hands. "We're all going," echoed Nadia behind him. "We're all going to tell them. We'll all stand there."

Her face was gathered in now, tucked in toward a center, an estimated longitude, which ran from the middle of her forehead to her chin and projected a cool resolution to annihilate any trace of self-pity. Her blond quiff fluttered above all that like a flag erected on a hilltop by the victor.

Matti scanned the empty lot around him. "Where's Adnan?" he suddenly thought to ask. "They took him in for questioning at the police," said Peninit. "They'll let him go, for sure. They have nothing on him, nothing, why wouldn't they let him go?"

Matti looked at his mother and sensed his regular, anticipatory anger giving way to a sort of compassion. His heart suddenly ached for her neck folds, which quivered and dripped with sweat, for her robbed, lost gaze and that unraveling of her expression, which made him think of a house after a burglary. "But he did us a favor," he said gently. She shrugged her shoulders, holding Arieh's hand. "Whatever you think. We're going," she said, but she did not move, remorseful for a moment. Then she turned to Nadia: "You don't have to come with us, really. Stay here, get some rest."

"Yes, yes," Ilan quickly concurred. He wiped Nadia's forehead with the turquoise sash that had been wrapped around his head. "You shouldn't go there. We'll tell the people everything."

"What everything?" Nadia panicked. "What 'everything'? Don't you dare tell them everything."

"That's a good idea, actually, for Ilan to come with us instead of you," Peninit intervened. "He'll come with us to the catering hall as the family representative and you take a pill and go get some sleep."

"Okay," Nadia acquiesced, though a look of doubt spread over her face. The words "family representative" kept working inside her, excreting sour juices of displeasure and disagreement. She also suspected that Peninit's goodwill was meant solely to soften her up before the inevitable blow: her obligation to help cover the deposit paid to the event hall.

Ilan cut off her labyrinth of contemplations. "I'm putting

something on, I'll be right down," he declared, and sprinted toward the building.

Arieh glanced at his watch. "Almost six," he announced gloomily. Arieh, Peninit, Nadia, and Matti sat down next to one another on the bench next to Gramsy, resembling a row of passengers on the back seat of a bus, waiting for Ilan. Waiting again. Except that now their expectation had a different flavor, chalky and bitter. (Matti stood up and moved to the curb, having almost been pushed off the crowded bench.) The black-and-white stray cat lay on the sidewalk, glaring at them gravely and somewhat curiously.

Evening had almost fallen when Ilan finally returned, stood opposite the bench and saluted. He was wearing Margie's old army uniform (he'd had a seamstress take it in awhile ago, to fit his gaunt figure), complete with the red beret on his head and the white socks folded carefully over black ankle boots. The khaki shirt was too tight on his chest, disclosing a hint of a bra line through the open top button, and it was tucked tightly into the narrow skirt that reached his knees, exposing his thin, shaved calves. He was radiant. His face glowed through a layer of makeup and his eyelids shimmered under glittery eye shadow.

"That's how you're going?" Matti broke the silence.

"Why not? What's wrong?" Ilan asked boldly and looked straight at Matti with a startled yet impudent stare. "With this kind of thing it's best to have someone in uniform. It helps people to see someone in uniform with this kind of thing."

"What kind of thing?" Matti demanded, tightening his hands into fists inside his pants pockets. "What kind of thing are you babbling about, where you need someone in uniform? Huh?"

"All right, leave him alone," Peninit said, getting up and digging around with her bare foot for the shoe she'd removed under the bench. "What difference does it make? He likes the uniform, so there'll be a uniform. Who knows, maybe he's right and it'll calm the atmosphere down a bit."

Nadia approached Ilan, felt the collar of his army shirt and sniffed at it. "Did you at least wash it?" she asked. Ilan proudly rolled up his sleeves to show her the shiny, clean cuffs. "I ironed, too! Look how I ironed."

They walked to the car. Arieh and Peninit sat in front (Peninit was driving), while Matti and Ilan shared the back-seat, each shrinking into his own corner, next to his own window.

They drove for almost ten minutes in a darkness that grew thicker and thicker until the cars honking at them conveyed to Peninit that she'd forgotten to turn her headlights on. "What do they want? What . . ," she mumbled angrily, glancing in the rearview mirror. "I look terrible. When you see a person looking like this, they don't need to say much."

Arieh receded into himself like an unused glove puppet, occupying less and less space in his seat. When he looked at Peninit for a moment, he anxiously noticed that the pierced hole in her earlobe was stretched down, reaching almost to the edge of the lobe, tearing under the weight of her earring. "We left all the bags at Nadia's," he said, apparently to himself.

Peninit passed a garbage truck that was dallying in front of her. "I want you to call your brother now," she said to Arieh.

"My brother? Why would I do that? We don't talk, I haven't talked to him in months!"

She looked straight ahead and sped up. "Call him, tell him what happened, and settle with him quickly about your mother's house. No lawyers. Call him now."

"But you were against it, all this time you were against the arrangement. What happened now that you're not against it? What happened?"

"What happened?" She screeched to a stop at a pedestrian crossing where a biker suddenly popped out onto the street. "A hundred thousand shekels happened. That's what happened. Our debt to that character from the catering hall, Mano Dvir, that's what happened. Will you be able to sleep at night if we take money from Nadia? Because I won't." She took a deep breath, looking around for something. "Where are the cigarettes?"

"What cigarettes?" Arieh asked boldly, in a soft voice. "You don't smoke."

"I'll pay for it," came Matti's voice from the backseat. "I'll pay you back the money."

"With what?" Peninit bellowed with false laughter, tilting her head back. "With what exactly will you pay us back? From your job at the phone company?"

No one said anything. Arieh gave a cautious glance at Peninit's tensely limp yet dense profile hunched over the wheel, at her fleshy lower lip, drooping and flaccid, which gave her the appearance of a child who'd been irredeemably insulted. His eyes were moist, stinging with tiredness, and an unfamiliar longing for something he could not identify suddenly washed over Arieh, filling him with new tenderness toward himself and this woman. "Maybe I should drive?" he said. "You rest a little, I'll drive." But Peninit merely tightened her grip on the wheel.

Hours later, when Matti woke up on the living room couch in Nadia's apartment (the cognac-colored, imitation leather perspired beneath him) it was one a.m., and as he looked at his watch twice, to make sure, he had the lazy thought (he was still climbing out of a bad sleep) that this hour was quite suited to itself. That it was entirely, and unusually, located in its appropriate age and date.

He kept lying on the couch, looking at the big dark window across the room, listening to the silence (Nadia had taken two sleeping pills) that strangely heightened the unique, undefinable, evocatively rich smell of the apartment. It was a blend of aromas that contained allusions and hints, mere hints and allusions at different smells, which slipped away and evaporated the moment they were defined: musk, fried eggplant, pungent cleaning solvents, dampness, lavender-scented air freshener, blossoming jasmine or magnolia ("What is magnolia?" he wondered.), vinegar, muscle rub, boiled milk, nail polish remover, the sour sweat of shoes, turmeric, rose water, and another element that sometimes reminded him of the smell of fresh printing and sometimes of the lucid, frozen no-smell of snow.

Matti shut his eyes, forced himself to shut them so he could concentrate, so he could finally figure out that smell, dig and dig all the way to its bottom, until he reached it, until his comprehension reached it and clarified it once and for all. He forged ahead, tensely accompanied by a feeling of something hugely fateful, as though cracking the code of this smell was tantamount to the locked door, to the most essential essence of the bedroom door that was still, to this moment, locked. What had Margie eaten all this time? He wondered what food she'd had, if any. He smiled in the darkness and the waffle-weave blanket tickled his nostrils: Margie eating a sandwich.

He ran the scene before his eyes in slow motion and in black and white, for some reason. Margie eating a sandwich she'd bought at the cafeteria on campus. First, with slender and cautious fingers, she slowly unwraps the thin plastic, then separates the two slices of bread. Then it all starts, the meticulous process of removing, cleaning, and exterminating. She removes the slices of tomato—throws them into the plastic bag next to her. Picks off the strips of lettuce smeared with mayonnaise, one by one—throws them in the bag. Takes out the sliced, pitted olives—tosses them. Removes the slices of cheese to reveal the cucumber underneath, picks them off— tosses them. Finally, with great attention, she uses a paper napkin to wipe off the edges of the sandwich and remove any trace of mayonnaise, examines the remaining object from all angles, slaps the two halves of the sandwich back together and begins to eat, looking up with her lustrous eyes to find his astonished look. And she says: "A person who eats a sandwich like that can do anything. Anything, right?"

Matti shook the blanket off, sat up, gathered the blanket and pillow in his arms and padded barefoot down the hallway to the locked door. He dropped the blanket and pillow to the floor, stood with his forehead on the door, eyes closed. A slight whiff of furniture polish (he added it to the list of components) and something else, reminiscent of vanilla and not unlike candy (marshmallow?) reached his nostrils. He felt a sharp pang in his chest, but it was on the right side, and it passed after a few seconds, leaving a trail of anxiety and emptiness. "Margie," he said very quietly, not to be heard but rather to make sure his throat and vocal chords were producing a sound, that they were capable of producing sound, even though the sound was full of strangeness to him now, strangeness upon strangeness, which reached out and joined up with the strangeness of that woman behind the door, who was his beloved—of course she was. Of course. Because it was thanks to her, or thanks to the strangeness actually, that she had become his beloved, and that was exactly what he loved about her, actually: her strangeness. He wriggled the toes of his bare feet, lifted them up, and put them back down. His loneliness was immeasurable. He bent down, arranged the pillow on the floor tiles, adjacent to the locked door, lay down and covered himself with the blanket, curled up on his side. The floor's hard, cold touch on his ribs was strangely pleasing. It felt right. For a moment it occurred to him that this slumber on the floor was the only one of all the slumbers that he hadn't stolen, that he didn't have to steal now, didn't have to earn dishonestly since it was being given to him justly, with precisely the right measure of generosity and justice, because it contained precise coordination, an appropriate suitability, between what was inside and what was outside.

Through the crack under the door came the smell of something again, the same something that contained a hint of a suggestion of the aroma of a package of candy, rustling paper streaked with chocolate.

Matti opened his eyes at once, listening to a memory narrated in Margie's voice, which reached him from beyond many distances, beyond the years even, many more years than he had known her. It was the voice she had always had, even before him: "Every afternoon, Nadia buys a piece of candy for Natalie. Every day, since she disappeared. Every day a different kind of candy. In the afternoon she buys the candy at the corner store and waits till evening and then till night. Only at night, when Natalie still hasn't come back, Nadia hides the candy in the linen box under her bed. There are dozens of candies in that box. Sometimes hundreds. Nadia arranges them by type, in neat piles. First the candy bars: Kif Kaf, Pesek Zman, Egozi. Then a pile of Red Cow chocolate bars. A pile of rum-flavored Tortit, and one of Mekupelet chocolates. Pile after pile, one next to the other. Once every month or two she empties out the box, shoves the candy into trash bags and leaves them out on the street, by the trash cans. A few times she didn't empty the candy out from the linen box for a few months and there was a horrible smell. Cockroaches. Ants. But in the last few years she's been emptying it. Forcing herself to. And those days in between when she empties the box and when it gets filled up again are the absolute most, you could say. The absolute most. They're not days at all, actually. They're not nights, either. I don't know what to call those days, I just know their color: black. But actually it's not black, either. Not even black. They have no color. Their color is no-color."

Shortly after Matti fell asleep on the floor next to the door (on the verge of falling asleep he found himself running his finger along the gap between the door and the floor, twice, back and forth, saying, "Good night, Margie"), he woke suddenly when he heard the front door being shut very softly. He got up quickly with the blanket and pillow and fled to the bathroom, where he sat down on the little carpet by the sink, hugged the pillow, and waited.

There were sounds of footsteps and whispers, at times swallowed up in the night's silence, at other times emerging in a slightly different format, a different syntax. There was a squeak that sounded like furniture being dragged, a muffled giggle, and padding feet again. Ilan and Gramsy appeared in the hallway. Gramsy was supported by Ilan, who held the stool in his other hand.

Gramsy was covered from head to toe in a large, white flannel nightgown, which gave her round body the heavy rectangular shape of a fridge, and her head was wrapped in a purple scarf. Ilan had changed only his army boots to plastic flip-flops. His long, black, greasy hair, which was usually tied in a ponytail, was loose now, falling in thick waves on his shoulders, covering the sides of his face and leaving only the middle third bare, with his thin, sensitive, prominent nose jutting out like an antenna. He held Gramsy by the armpits and sat her down heavily on the stool. Then he knelt down at her feet and put his head on her lap, his cheek resting on her broad thighs. (Matti peeked at them and slipped away, dropping the pillow and blanket on the living room couch on his way out of the apartment.)

Gramsy tipped her head back, cupped one hand to her ear and started singing. At first her voice was very soft, like a hum or a buzz, but it slowly grew louder, repeating the same refrain over and over again like an instrument warming up, seeking the right path. She tried out the opening line of Fairuz's *"Khayef aqul ili fi'albi,"* paused, then started again in a different scale: "I'm afraid to say what's in my heart." After a few moments, her voice found the right verse in the right key, started again, and this time completed the whole chorus:

> *Khayef aqul ili fi'albi*
> *Titkal w-t'aned w'yaya*
> *Walav dareit anaq khubi tifd'hkni eini b'hawaya . . .*

Gramsy looked straight ahead at the shut door, her eyes

almost popping out of their sockets from aiming at it, and sang. And sang. Her voice grew louder, fuller, ripening from moment to moment in its crystal-clear trill, gathered into itself yet simultaneously so very open, wide open to the world, directed not at one single listener but at many listeners, who all seemed to gather under the broad wingspan of her voice, assembling there as though they'd been waiting for a long time for this voice to bring them together.

> *I'm afraid to say what is in my heart*
> *So that your heart does not harden*
> *And you become stubborn with me*

Her voice climbed up, filling and melting the space of the narrow hallway. Then it invaded the other areas of the apartment (through her heavy sleep, the voice touched Nadia's ears and her hand lifted up slightly, as if to brush away a mosquito), filled them and ripened them, and finally spread out into the muggy air of the nighttime neighborhood, through the other apartment windows, the power lines stretched out between the tall hot-water tanks on the rooftops, the old antennas, the two lookout towers atop the shopping center, and the gaps of air between the buildings.

"Khayef aqul ili fi'albi, titkal w't'aned w'yaya..." Grandma's voice curled up and insisted for an instant on the *w't'aned*, as though seeking to oppose the song's stubborn

man with her own stubbornness, to encircle him with melodic stubbornness, which was in fact nothing but massive and wonderful tenderness, at times pure and innocent, at times sly, circuitous, twirling. Gramsy rocked on the stool as she sang, back and forth, digging her fingers through Ilan's hair on her lap. She cupped her hand over her ear again to clarify her voice and return it into herself, only to gather up strength and erupt again, *"Khayef aqul ili fi'albi"*—"I'm afraid to say what is in my heart," until suddenly, from inside and through Gramsy's singing, there came a creaking sound from behind the door, then pushing, dragging, pulling, drawers loudly opening, glass bottles clanging.

The key turned in the lock. Once, then once more. Then it waited.

RONIT MATALON (1959–2017) was the author of nine novels and a liberal social activist. The daughter of Egyptian immigrants to Israel, she worked as a journalist for the newspaper *Haaretz* and reported from the West Bank and Gaza. Her last book, *And the Bride Closed the Door,* was awarded Israel's prestigious Brenner Prize the day before her death at age 58.

JESSICA COHEN shared the 2017 Man Booker International Prize with author David Grossman for her translation of *A Horse Walks Into a Bar.* She has translated works by Amos Oz, Etgar Keret, Dorit Rabinyan, Ronit Matalon and Nir Baram.

EXPOSED
BY JEAN-PHILIPPE BLONDEL

A dangerous intimacy emerges between a French teacher and a former student who has achieved art world celebrity. The painting of a portrait upturns both their lives. Jean-Philippe Blondel, author of the bestselling novel *The 6:41 to Paris,* evokes an intimacy of dangerous intensity in a stunning tale about aging, regret and moving ahead into the future.

THE 6:41 TO PARIS
BY JEAN-PHILIPPE BLONDEL

Cécile, a stylish 47-year-old, has spent the weekend visiting her parents outside Paris. By Monday morning, she's exhausted. These trips back home are stressful and she settles into a train compartment with an empty seat beside her. But it's soon occupied by a man she recognizes as Philippe Leduc, with whom she had a passionate affair that ended in her brutal humiliation 30 years ago. In the fraught hour and a half that ensues, Cécile and Philippe hurtle towards the French capital in a psychological thriller about the pain and promise of past romance.

OBLIVION
BY SERGEI LEBEDEV

In one of the first 21st century Russian novels to probe the legacy of the Soviet prison camp system, a young man travels to the vast wastelands of the Far North to uncover the truth about a shadowy neighbor who saved his life, and whom he knows only as Grandfather II. Emerging from today's Russia, where the ills of the past are being forcefully erased from public memory, this masterful novel represents an epic literary attempt to rescue history from the brink of oblivion.

SOME DAY
BY SHEMI ZARHIN

On the shores of Israel's Sea of Galilee lies the city of Tiberias, a place bursting with sexuality and longing for love. The air is saturated with smells of cooking and passion. *Some Day* is a gripping family saga, a sensual and emotional feast that plays out over decades. This is an enchanting tale about tragic fates that disrupt families and break our hearts. Zarhin's hypnotic writing renders a painfully delicious vision of individual lives behind Israel's larger national story.

WHAT'S LEFT OF THE NIGHT
BY ERSI SOTIROPOULOS

Constantine Cavafy arrives in Paris in 1897 on a trip that will deeply shape his future and push him toward his poetic inclination. With this lyrical novel, tinged with an hallucinatory eroticism that unfolds over three unforgettable days, celebrated Greek author Ersi Sotiropoulos depicts Cavafy in the midst of a journey of self-discovery across a continent on the brink of massive change. A stunning portrait of a budding author—before he became C.P. Cavafy, one of the 20th century's greatest poets—that illuminates the complex relationship of art, life, and the erotic desires that trigger creativity.

ALEXANDRIAN SUMMER
BY YITZHAK GORMEZANO GOREN

This is the story of two Jewish families living their frenzied last days in the doomed cosmopolitan social whirl of Alexandria just before fleeing Egypt for Israel in 1951. The conventions of the Egyptian upper-middle class are laid bare in this dazzling novel, which exposes sexual hypocrisies and portrays a vanished polyglot world of horse racing, seaside promenades and nightclubs.

THE EYE
BY PHILIPPE COSTAMAGNA

It's a rare and secret profession, comprising a few dozen people around the world equipped with a mysterious mixture of knowledge and innate sensibility. Summoned to Swiss bank vaults, Fifth Avenue apartments, and Tokyo storerooms, they are entrusted by collectors, dealers, and museums to decide if a coveted picture is real or fake and to determine if it was painted by Leonardo da Vinci or Raphael. *The Eye* lifts the veil on the rarified world of connoisseurs devoted to the authentication and discovery of Old Master artworks.

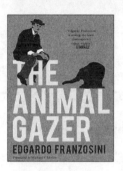

THE ANIMAL GAZER
BY EDGARDO FRANZOSINI

A hypnotic novel inspired by the strange and fascinating life of sculptor Rembrandt Bugatti, brother of the fabled automaker. Bugatti obsessively observes and sculpts the baboons, giraffes, and panthers in European zoos, finding empathy with their plight and identifying with their life in captivity. Rembrandt Bugatti's work, now being rediscovered, is displayed in major art museums around the world and routinely fetches large sums at auction. Edgardo Franzosini recreates the young artist's life with intense lyricism, passion, and sensitivity.

ALLMEN AND THE DRAGONFLIES
BY MARTIN SUTER

Johann Friedrich von Allmen has exhausted his family fortune by living in Old World grandeur despite present-day financial constraints. Forced to downscale, Allmen inhabits the garden house of his former Zurich estate, attended by his Guatemalan butler, Carlos. This is the first of a series of humorous, fast-paced detective novels devoted to a memorable gentleman thief. A thrilling art heist escapade infused with European high culture and luxury that doesn't shy away from the darker side of human nature.

The Madeleine Project
by Clara Beaudoux

A young woman moves into a Paris apartment and discovers a storage room filled with the belongings of the previous owner, a certain Madeleine who died in her late nineties, and whose treasured possessions nobody seems to want. In an audacious act of journalism driven by personal curiosity and humane tenderness, Clara Beaudoux embarks on *The Madeleine Project*, documenting what she finds on Twitter with text and photographs, introducing the world to an unsung 20th century figure.

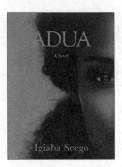

Adua
by Igiaba Scego

Adua, an immigrant from Somalia to Italy, has lived in Rome for nearly forty years. She came seeking freedom from a strict father and an oppressive regime, but her dreams of film stardom ended in shame. Now that the civil war in Somalia is over, her homeland calls her. She must decide whether to return and reclaim her inheritance, but also how to take charge of her own story and build a future.

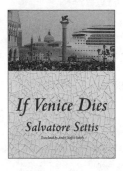

If Venice Dies
by Salvatore Settis

Internationally renowned art historian Salvatore Settis ignites a new debate about the Pearl of the Adriatic and cultural patrimony at large. In this fiery blend of history and cultural analysis, Settis argues that "hit-and-run" visitors are turning Venice and other landmark urban settings into shopping malls and theme parks. This is a passionate plea to secure the soul of Venice, written with consummate authority, wide-ranging erudition and élan.

THE MADONNA OF NOTRE DAME
BY ALEXIS RAGOUGNEAU

Fifty thousand people jam into Notre Dame Cathedral to celebrate the Feast of the Assumption. The next morning, a beautiful young woman clothed in white kneels at prayer in a cathedral side chapel. But when someone accidentally bumps against her, her body collapses. She has been murdered. This thrilling novel illuminates shadowy corners of the world's most famous cathedral, shedding light on good and evil with suspense, compassion and wry humor.

THE LAST WEYNFELDT
BY MARTIN SUTER

Adrian Weynfeldt is an art expert in an international auction house, a bachelor in his mid-fifties living in a grand Zurich apartment filled with costly paintings and antiques. Always correct and well-mannered, he's given up on love until one night—entirely out of character for him—Weynfeldt decides to take home a ravishing but unaccountable young woman and gets embroiled in an art forgery scheme that threatens his buttoned up existence. This refined page-turner moves behind elegant bourgeois facades into darker recesses of the heart.

MOVING THE PALACE
BY CHARIF MAJDALANI

A young Lebanese adventurer explores the wilds of Africa, encountering an eccentric English colonel in Sudan and enlisting in his service. In this lush chronicle of far-flung adventure, the military recruit crosses paths with a compatriot who has dismantled a sumptuous palace and is transporting it across the continent on a camel caravan. This is a captivating modern-day Odyssey in the tradition of Bruce Chatwin and Paul Theroux.

ON THE RUN WITH MARY
BY JONATHAN BARROW

Shining moments punctuate this story of a youth
on the run after escaping from an elite English
boarding school. At London's Euston Station, the
narrator meets a talking dachshund named Mary
and together they're off on escapades through
posh Mayfair streets and jaunts in a Rolls-Royce.
But the youth soon realizes that the seemingly
sweet dog is an alcoholic, nymphomaniac, drug-
addicted mess. *On the Run with Mary* mirrors the horrors and the joys of
the terrible 20th century.

THE LAST SUPPER
BY KLAUS WIVEL

Alarmed by the oppression of 7.5 million
Christians in the Middle East, journalist Klaus
Wivel traveled to Iraq, Lebanon, Egypt, and
the Palestinian territories to learn about their
fate. He found a minority under threat of death
and humiliation, desperate in the face of rising
Islamic extremism and without hope their
situation will improve. An unsettling account
of a severely beleaguered religious group living, so it seems, on borrowed
time. Wivel asks, Why have we not done more to protect these people?

GUYS LIKE ME
BY DOMINIQUE FABRE

Dominique Fabre, born in Paris and a life-
long resident of the city, exposes the shadowy,
anonymous lives of many who inhabit the French
capital. In this quiet, subdued tale, a middle-aged
office worker, divorced and alienated from his
only son, meets up with two childhood friends
who are similarly adrift. He's looking for a second
act to his mournful life, seeking the harbor of
love and a true connection with his son. Set in palpably real Paris streets
that feel miles away from the City of Light, a stirring novel of regret and
absence, yet not without a glimmer of hope.

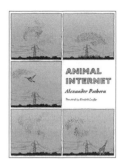

ANIMAL INTERNET
BY ALEXANDER PSCHERA

Some 50,000 creatures around the globe—including whales, leopards, flamingoes, bats and snails—are being equipped with digital tracking devices. The data gathered and studied by major scientific institutes about their behavior will warn us about tsunamis, earthquakes and volcanic eruptions, but also radically transform our relationship to the natural world. Contrary to pessimistic fears, author Alexander Pschera sees the Internet as creating a historic opportunity for a new dialogue between man and nature.

KILLING AUNTIE
BY ANDRZEJ BURSA

A young university student named Jurek, with no particular ambitions or talents, finds himself with nothing to do. After his doting aunt asks the young man to perform a small chore, he decides to kill her for no good reason other than, perhaps, boredom. This short comedic masterpiece combines elements of Dostoevsky, Sartre, Kafka, and Heller, coming together to produce an unforgettable tale of murder and—just maybe—redemption.

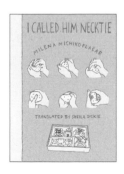

I CALLED HIM NECKTIE
BY MILENA MICHIKO FLAŠAR

Twenty-year-old Taguchi Hiro has spent the last two years of his life living as a hikikomori—a shut-in who never leaves his room and has no human interaction—in his parents' home in Tokyo. As Hiro tentatively decides to reenter the world, he spends his days observing life from a park bench. Gradually he makes friends with Ohara Tetsu, a salaryman who has lost his job. The two discover in their sadness a common bond. This beautiful novel is moving, unforgettable, and full of surprises.

New Vessel Press

*To purchase these titles and for more information
please visit newvesselpress.com.*